ISBN - 13: 9781989698983

Give feedback on the book at:
lorhainneeckhart@hotmail.com

Twitter: @LEckhart
Facebook: AuthorLorhainneEckhart

Printed in the U.S.A

THE DATING GAME

The Parker Sisters

LORHAINNE ECKHART

The Parker Sisters

The Parker Sisters, a spinoff of the romance series
Married in Montana from a Readers' Favorite award—
winning author and "queen of the family saga"
(Aherman)

The Parker Sisters
Thrill of the Chase
The Dating Game
Play Hard to Get
What We Can't Have
Go Your Own Way
A June Wedding

Thrill of the Chase: *He stopped for an accident and stumbled upon the one woman he'd been looking for all his life.*

The Dating Game: A sexy single nurse looking for love. Two handsome, eligible men quickly step up, but one of them is a total mystery. Can she solve the puzzle and figure out which one is Mr. Right?

Playing Hard to Get: Twenty-four-year-old Naomi Parker is interning as a journalist when she stumbles onto a big story about a ruthless man, a destroyer of women. With two objectives in mind, to be the best she can be and to not let him find out who she really is, Naomi sets out to uncover everything Cameron Donnelly has been trying to hide. The only problem is that he might not be everything she believes him to be.

What We Can't Have: Seventeen year old Mason Parker has been keeping a secret from her family about the boy next door. And after a chance encounter, the timing all wrong, Mason and Justin are faced with a dilemma as considering being together, could end up dividing two families.

Go Your Own Way: Scarlett Parker has big plans for her life which don't include living the same life as her sisters or having anything to do with her father's ranch. Until one day she meets a man who is everything she is not. A man who belongs to no one and turns the tables on Scarlett, when she is suddenly the one who is being tamed.

A June Wedding: Dearly beloved, we are gathered in this month of June for a wedding at the Parker family ranch. Or so the invitation says! Little does the family know that not just one Parker sister is getting married, but three. Will this be the wedding of the season, or will three sisters end up with broken hearts?

From a Readers' Favorite award—winning author and "queen of the family saga" (Aherman) comes The Parker Sisters a new spinoff series of the Married in Montana series.

Dating can be confusing, especially when you have too many choices…and sometimes the mystery can land you in the middle of a compelling romantic mystery.

A sexy single nurse looking for love. Two handsome, eligible men quickly step up, but one of them is a total mystery. Can she solve the puzzle and figure out which one is Mr. Right?

"Damn, she looks beautiful," said twenty-six-year-old Ivy Parker. She couldn't keep her eyes from the scene in front of her: her sister Taz on the makeshift dance floor in the arms of her husband of five hours, Jerry O'Rourke—and man, could he dance.

Taz's white gown swept the floor, cut low in the back and front, and her dark hair was pinned up with orchids. Jerry was dashing in his elegant black tux, and for the first time it hit Ivy how right they looked together. It was a happy thought that left her feeling so sad and lonely.

"Happy too, the bitch," said Naomi, her sister, who was also a bridesmaid and very much as single as Ivy. The two stood in identical peach gowns that draped to their ankles. The only problem was that the dress looked better on all her sisters' slender frames, whereas it seemed to add at least twenty pounds to Ivy's size ten—okay, maybe twelve if she was being honest. She'd finally stopped looking in the mirror, horrified at how the dress looked like a grain sack on her and made her ass look far bigger than she knew it was. Another reason, she was sure, that she was fighting to keep a smile pasted to her face.

"What are you two going on about?" said Brandyne, their eldest sister, as she slipped in between them and put her arms around them. Her dark hair was long and wavy to her slim waist, and her wedding ring was the first thing Ivy had noticed of late. Brandyne was married to a Montana sheriff, with five kids from a cowboy she'd hooked up with years before. She too was slender and curvy. Damn, so unfair.

"Oh, you know, our sister over there dancing with Jerry. Still can't believe she's married, and so soon after meeting the guy. She traded us all in and left us, just like you," Ivy said. She glanced over her shoulder to Brandyne, who seemed a little startled. Naomi too gave her an odd look. She shrugged. "Sorry, just things are changing faster than…" She stopped talking when Brandyne and Naomi's disapproving glares turned darker.

"Boy, are you ever in a funk," Brandyne said, and Naomi nodded in agreement. "Shake it off. This is Taz's day. I hope to all hell you didn't lay any of this at her feet?"

"No, of course not. I smiled and did everything I was supposed to as the maid of honor: fussed over her, did her nails, got her some sexy underwear with garters and an indecent lacy push-up bra. Jerry's going to go weak at the knees when he pulls her dress off tonight. I even provided the necessary shot of whiskey when Daddy showed up to lead her down the aisle and I saw the panic about to take hold at what she'd gotten herself into."

Her sisters were still looking at her oddly. She decided it was best to leave out the part where she'd offered to drive the getaway car just in case the last-minute jitters and panic attack were Taz's intuition's way of stepping up to warn her about the giant mistake she was about to make.

No, she figured that part would likely get her a scolding from just about everyone, considering even Taz had burst into laughter, believing the offer was Ivy's sense of humor gone wild. It wasn't, but Ivy noted painfully that it had been the confidence boost her sister needed to get up, take her father's arm, and practically skip down the aisle to say "I do."

Scarlett, their seventeen-year-old sister, bounced to Ivy's other side. She was in a party mood. "OMG, have you seen all the hot guys Jerry invited? I swear this is the most fun I've ever had and the best party this county has ever seen." Her short dark hair was growing out but still made her round cheeks and bold, mischievous eyes really pop. Then she set her hand over her heart in such a dramatic way. "I still can't believe she's married and living in Denver, and there's now, what, four of us left? Wonder what Daddy and Mama will do with Taz's cottage?"

From her expression, Ivy could see the calculations going on in Scarlett's mind. She was over-the-top dramatic about everything and was always looking for the angle, for what was best for her.

"Do you think Daddy will let me have it?" she said. There it was, all about her.

"Yeah, don't think so, Scarlett," Ivy said as she took in all the guests, three hundred neighbors, friends, and distant cousins along with a few of Jerry's family and business associates—hence the drop-dead gorgeous guys with hot babes on their arms. Her parents were also now on the dance floor. Riske, the live band Jerry had brought in, were clients of his and were currently at the top of the charts, another reason Scarlett was beside herself. They were good and loud.

"You know what, Ivy? Your turn will come," Brandyne said. "You'll find your Mr. Right, your perfect partner, and then you'll be the one up there looking so happy and over the moon."

Ivy couldn't even pretend to believe a word she was saying, so she just grunted. Unlike Scarlett, Ivy hated being the center of attention and anyone making a fuss over her.

"Looks like Mama's having a great time," Brandyne said. "Haven't seen her laugh like that in a long while."

Her dad was a pretty good dancer, too, and her mom glowed in her cream dress, smiling and relaxed for the first time since the wedding plans had begun.

"You're right," Ivy said. "She was a wreck, worried and nervous right up until they said 'I do.' She's the wedding coordinator, the one who made this dog and pony show, as Daddy's put it several times over the past few weeks, a reality." She gestured to the magnificent huge tent that had arrived on a flatbed along with all of the tables and kitchen equipment the caterers needed at their disposal.

"This is awesome," Scarlett said. "Exactly how I want my wedding, lavish, expensive, all the flowers, the crystal, the meal served by waiters—but I'd also like ice sculptures and champagne, and white doves released just when we say 'I do.'" She pressed her hand to her chest, and Ivy was absolutely speechless. Apparently so were Naomi and Brandyne, who exchanged a look as if Scarlett had lost her mind.

"So anyone know where they're off to on their honeymoon?" Ivy said. She hadn't a clue, and Taz had said it was a surprise. Jerry wouldn't even tell her whether she needed a bikini or a parka, just that they'd be flying off after the reception tonight and he'd taken care of packing her things.

"Can I have your attention, please?" the emcee said. "I need all the single women up here on the dance floor. The bride is going to be throwing the bouquet. All you single guys, don't worry. Your turn's coming up next."

A hand wrapped around her wrist. "Come on, Ivy." It was Mason, their youngest sister, her hair dyed strawberry red to match the dress, she said, though Ivy thought it clashed with the peach.

Mason pulled her into the already crowded dance floor, which was packed with all the single women of Kaycee. Ivy slipped to the back, hoping to hide and make her way out of the tent into the dark. She peeked around Martha, the town's thin and reedy librarian, who had thick glasses and an overbite, to see the closest opening. Everyone was counting, and she was being shoved by Tina, the drugstore clerk, thirty and single, who was literally fisting her hands and flexing her muscles, obviously prepared to take down anyone who got between her and that bouquet. Tina shouted something, pumping her fist in the air, which had Ivy taking a step to the side and squeezing through the women pushing behind her.

She was shoved and then bumped, her foot stepped on as she slinked to the edge of the tent. She could see Brandyne and her handsome sheriff husband, Blake, laughing at the sidelines, most likely at the crazed women all determined to be the one to catch that bouquet, as if it were any guarantee that person would actually be next to marry. What a stupid tradition! Ivy wanted no part of it.

"Two!" she heard the emcee shout from the stage.

The women were all screaming, and she was one step closer to freedom and sanity. She lifted her dress as her feet pinched in the ridiculously high sandals she'd squeezed them into. The women were going nuts. She was elbowed from behind and grabbed a chair when she nearly lost her balance. "Excuse me, sorry about that," she muttered to who she thought was Irene, the owner of the local bar, in her late forties.

"One!"

She stepped to the edge of the tent.

"Ivy Parker, would you stand still so I can throw these flowers your way? Get on back here," Taz yelled out, and everyone turned to face her where she stood, one high-heeled foot on the dirt outside the tent and one on the makeshift floor that would be gone the next day. She wanted to kill her sister as she gestured to cut it out.

Too late. Everyone was looking her way as the flowers flew in a near perfect line drive and hit her in the face. She grabbed them only to preserve her dignity as she stumbled back. She was sure her heels would break, her ankle twisting. Warm large hands gripped her waist.

"Whoa, there," the man said. He had a deep voice and was tall, dark haired, and totally ripped, from what she could tell in the navy suit he wore. His tie was loosened, and he was strong, judging by the way he lifted her as if she weighed nothing and set her back on her feet.

"Yeah…" She couldn't think of what else to say, holding a bouquet, hearing her sisters in the background and ignoring every one of them. She felt stupid. He was rough and gorgeous, not pretty but hard, chiseled, now smiling at her as if teasing her.

He glanced over her head and let his hand fall from her waist. "Think you're being summoned." He gestured with his chin.

"Ivy, get on back here!" Taz said, now holding the mic. Ivy wanted to kick her as she shook her head, intent on getting the hell out of there. She was done with this spectacle and refused to be dragged to the center of the floor to be displayed as a spinster, to have it pointed out to everyone that hey, just maybe she was next, as if being single were something to be ashamed of.

"I think they want you back there," he said. She was sure now she could hear the laughter in his voice.

"Yeah, no, I think not," she said and laughed, then nearly cringed at the giddy sound in her voice. She didn't do giddy. What the hell?

He was still smiling, and the light touched his amber eyes. He had long lashes for a guy. Who'd have thought they would make him that much hotter? She was envious. Then a hand gripped her arm and she was yanked away.

"Scarlett, let go of me," she said and batted at her. Scarlett was unbelievably strong. Flower petals fell to the floor around them.

"Since you just had to catch the bouquet, you know the tradition. You're now next to get married. So you just stand here like a good girl and wait for the guys' turn."

Ivy could hear the jealousy spitting from her sister and wanted to correct her about all of it. "You know what? You take it. It's all yours. I'll just get on out of here." She tried to hand the flowers over, but Scarlett gave her the flat of her hand.

"Too late," she said and left Ivy to stand like an idiot, alone on the dance floor.

The few guys who stepped up cheered and hollered as Taz lifted her leg on a stool and Jerry lifted her skirt, showing her bare leg and the garter on her thigh. He slipped it off her leg, balled it in his fist, and tossed it. The five men there all jumped, and time stood still.

A hand in the air held the garter, and the men parted to reveal the brown tweed and pot belly of Vern Butterfield, the seventy-year-old widower from the next spread over.

"Good God," she heard Naomi hiss from behind her.

Then she was pushed to the center of the floor as Vern made the face of a man who'd had too much to drink and had just won the lottery as he strutted toward her. The band started up, and he grabbed her hand.

"Hey, my lucky night," he said. "Guess this dance is mine." He stank of one too many beers as he rested a sweaty hand on the small of her back, whipping her around as if he could dance, which he couldn't. He just jumped with two left feet.

All she could think was that this was about as bad as it could get.

Chapter Two

Ivy pulled her strappy high-heeled sandals from her swollen feet. They had looked great in the window of the shoe shop in Buffalo, but after two hours, her feet had had enough. After nine, she was ready to crawl as she walked like an old woman over to the round table where her sisters were sitting, laughing. Waiters were clearing away dishes and food, packing up everything else.

Brandyne was laughing, perched on Blake's lap, her arm around him, looking happier than Ivy had ever seen her.

"My God, I don't think I can walk another step," she said as she took the end chair between Naomi and Mason. Brandyne's eldest daughter, sixteen-year-old Rita, was also there, looking pretty in a deep blue off-the-shoulder cocktail dress.

"Here, have a beer. It'll take the edge off," Naomi said as she slid a bottle over.

"Did they get away okay?" Ivy asked. She lifted the beer, which was lukewarm, and took a swallow, fighting the urge to make a face. She hated warm beer.

"They just left along with the last of the guests. Limo was taking them into Buffalo," Blake said, one hand possessively on Brandyne's ass, the other holding a beer. He was such a handsome man, rough looking, a scar at the edge of his strong square jaw. She realized he had that badass look, kind of like the stranger she'd bumped into earlier and hadn't seen since. Who was he?

"So anyone know where Jerry is taking our sister for her honeymoon?" Naomi asked.

Ivy took in the dark blue label on her beer bottle, still thinking of the stranger's wide chest. Again, who the hell was he?

Brandyne tipped back her beer and glanced to her husband. "Blake knows but hasn't told me, just said he couldn't, so stop asking."

"Hey, I told you already that Jerry asked me to keep it quiet. He didn't want Taz to know, and he seemed to think one of you would spill it."

She wasn't sure who said what to Blake, but Mason, Naomi, and Scarlett all protested, and one tossed a napkin his way. Brandyne was shaking her head, still leaning against him.

"Suppose it's safe to say now since they're gone, though," he said. Yup, he had a killer smile, too, just like that mystery guy. What was it with these badass types? They were so far from the clean-cut guy she should have been looking for.

"So is it a beach or Alaska?" Naomi asked.

Ivy pushed the beer away. It was tasteless, and she was beginning to feel a headache kicking in. Water, she needed water.

"Neither," he said.

What? They all looked at one another, trying to figure out what was left.

"Blake, I heard you say a train," Rita said as she leaned around her mom.

"You only heard part of it." Blake gestured sternly to Rita with his finger. "But good on you for not saying anything until now," he added with a smile.

"So spill, Blake. Where is Jerry taking our sister?" Scarlett tapped the table.

"To the UK for a train trip on the Royal Scotsman, then off to Italy, France, and Greece for three weeks." He rested his beer on the table, and the look on his face seemed distant for a second. Ivy wasn't sure what to make of it. "That would be a once-in-a-lifetime trip for some, way out of my price range." He was looking at Brandyne, and she got it then: regret or something.

Brandyne put her beer down and flattened her hand over his chest, rubbing intimately. "Yeah, well, who wants Europe, anyway? I have everything I want right here."

Everyone was quiet, and for a moment she felt as if she were intruding on a private moment between her sister and Blake. They were so in love, and he was so devoted to her and to her kids. A good man. She swallowed the longing.

"Well, I want Europe," Scarlett said. "Lucky Taz. One day I swear I'm going to travel the world, see it all, visit castles and queens and…"

"Scarlett, you still have school to finish. Get a job and get back to reality," Naomi said.

"And it's your turn to wash the floor tomorrow," Mason said, jabbing the plastic drink sword she was playing with at her sister. Then she reached for Ivy's beer and snuck a drink. Everyone looked, but no one said anything.

"Oh, pooh on all of you. I'll have it all just like Taz. Even more. She just happened to luck out, finding a rich guy, but mine, when I meet him, he'll be even more. He'll own the world," she added with her signature dramatic flair.

Even Blake frowned, his eyes narrowed as if he was deciding which category of trouble to stick Scarlett into.

When Mason lifted her beer to take another swallow, Ivy reached over and took it from her. "Don't think I don't know you've been sneaking all night, but cool it. Mama and Daddy will find out, and it's not just us here." She lowered her voice, knowing Blake was watching, listening.

"Your sister's right, Mason. You're too young," Blake said, glancing over to Rita as well. Then chairs scraped at the other end, and Brandyne, Rita, and Blake stood up. "It's getting late. We're going to turn in and find our other hooligans."

Everyone said goodnight. Scarlett left next, and then Naomi, leaving just Mason and Ivy in the tent with the waiters and staff, who would likely be cleaning up until the wee hours.

"So everyone's gone now. How about you and me raid the bar before they finish packing it up?" Mason whispered as Ivy's headache really kicked up.

"No, not tonight. I need water and then sleep, and…" As she started to get up, she cursed her swollen feet and dangled her ridiculously high uncomfortable shoes in one hand, leaning heavily on the table with the other. "A hot bath to soak my feet. Come on, get up. You can help me to my cabin."

She gestured to Mason, who sulked but was a good sport, as she let Ivy loop her arm over her shoulder and lean on her as they crept out of the tent. Pain shot up her legs. "Ow, ow, ow, not so fast," Ivy said.

Her sister laughed at her but led her across the property in the dirt. The area around the tent was lit up, but darkness loomed around the house and the three cottages built just fifty feet from it. Right now, as they made their way, giggling and stumbling, those few feet seemed to be a mile.

Chapter Three

S ensible shoes were a must, and even though she'd been on her feet for only a few hours today in the maternity ward, her white Nikes with extra cushiony support seemed to be giving way. Maybe her brutalized feet were still paying the price from the previous night's wedding.

"Heard Mrs. Holly is being prepped for a C-section," said Ivy's colleague, Gail. The woman had dark skin and was a few years older than Ivy, married with two kids, one of four floor nurses in the maternity ward.

"Yup, she's got Tucker for a doctor," Ivy said. "Slice and dice is his specialty. Think the guy gets off on cutting women open. Says it's safer, but I've never yet seen a mom in distress like he says could happen."

There was silence, and she had an awful feeling as she looked up to see Gail on the other side of the desk, her face pale, the air suddenly tense. She jumped and looked back to see Dr. Tucker behind her—tall, handsome, with light hair and a pissed-off expression. How could she have been so stupid?

"Slice and dice, seriously?" he said. "When, Ms. Parker, was it that you went to medical school and then interned and did a residency on the maternity ward?"

Holy shit, he was pissed. She'd have given anything at that point for the ground to open up and swallow her. "I'm sorry, I misspoke. Just tired is all," she said. He was still staring down on her when she thought she heard Gail excuse herself and slip away. Damn, couldn't she have warned her?

"So is that what you really think, that I'd put a mother in jeopardy with unnecessary surgery?"

Valid question, and one she didn't think she should answer truthfully. "Of course not, Doctor. Sorry again. Just seems a high number of your patients end up opting for a C-section instead of a natural birth, whereas Doctor Jennings is the opposite." What the hell was wrong with her? She needed to stop talking.

He stepped forward to the counter and leaned against it. Damn, he was attractive, clean cut, but he held no appeal for her. "Just so happens I have a perfect record. I've never lost a patient or a baby, and you'd better think twice about questioning my decisions or I'll make sure this is the last day you ever work in this hospital." Loud and clear. She felt ground into the dirt. "Do I make myself clear, or should I file a complaint with the head nurse?"

Now who was being an asshole? She went to speak when a hand touched her shoulder.

"Hey, there you are," Henry Blackwell, head of obstetrics, interrupted. "Can I borrow Ivy, Gus, or are you two in the middle of something?"

Dr. Tucker took a moment to pull his gaze from Ivy before shaking his head. "No, done with her," he said. He moved away but stopped, stepping back as if he'd remembered something. "If I ever hear you bad mouthing me again, Ivy, I'll make sure you don't work anywhere at all."

Then he was gone, and Ivy blew out a breath, knowing she'd just barely managed to ward off the trouble her mouth had created. "Thank you," she said to Henry, who was watching her and a retreating Doctor Tucker.

"Yeah, Gail said you'd dug yourself into a corner. She told me what you said. Seriously, Ivy, you have to watch your mouth. You can't go around saying stuff like that."

Dr. Blackwell wasn't much to look at. He wasn't overly tall, and he didn't have striking features. He did, though, have blue eyes and dark hair with a touch of gray. She figured he was in his early forties. She liked him.

"I'm sorry," she said. "I didn't know he was standing behind me, and I didn't really mean what I said."

He smiled. His gaze never left her, but the humor never reached his eyes. "Of course you did. We all think the same thing, but he has privileges. He's board certified, and there's nothing you or I can do about it."

"So you agree with me? Even Mrs. Holly hasn't been in labor all that long, seven hours. I've been monitoring, and there've been no signs for mom or baby that—"

"Stop talking, Ivy." Dr. Blackwell actually gestured for her to close her mouth. "His call, and the mom's. What we think and what's going to happen are two different things. Next time, Ivy, when you're tempted to question a doctor's decision, don't. That advice is from a friend. This next is from the head of OB. If he wanted to file a complaint against you, even if your allegations have merit, you would soon find yourself with no doctors wanting to work with you, and that would make you unemployable. Understand?"

"I get it," she said, and she did. She needed to stop

saying what she was thinking. It was something she'd been doing more and more as of late.

He rested his hand on her arm and rubbed. "I know you do. I like you, Ivy. I just don't want to see you get on the wrong side of someone here." He had a nice smile, too. He was still standing there, and for a minute she thought he wanted to say something else, ask her something else. "When are you finished your shift tonight?" he finally said.

"Midnight," she replied. Another four hours to go and then she could get off her feet and find a bath, a bed, and a book, the same as every night.

"Do you want to grab a bite or a drink with me?" he said. It was the way he asked, the way he was looking at her, that made her realize his interest. Not that she hadn't known he liked her, but she got the sense he was now putting something different out there.

"Okay," she said. Should she? She liked him, of course, but there just wasn't any of that off-the-charts chemistry or pull or attraction she'd have liked. He was nice, though, and she really did like talking to him.

"Great, why don't I pick you up here at the end of your shift? We'll have dinner and a drink."

"Who's going for a drink?" Gail appeared and looked between Henry and Ivy just as the phone buzzed. She answered and said, "Maternity. Yup, okay, buzz them in." She hung up and looked over. "New mom in labor on her way in. You want me to get them settled or you, Ivy?"

"I'll take her. Mine just went up for a C-section, so put her in room four." She heard the door buzz and a man's voice. The women he was with was breathing in the familiar manner of a woman in labor.

"Hey, there…" she started to say before she glanced up to see the hot badass she'd stumbled against the night before while trying to flee the tent. He had his arm around the pregnant woman. Of course he was taken. Someone with his looks wouldn't have been walking around unattached. That just wasn't reality. She realized he hadn't recognized her, but then, all of his attention was on the woman beside him, who had stopped and leaned over, hit by a contraction that looked as if it had sucked her breath away.

"Okay, let's get you into room four and find out how far you're dilated," Ivy said. As she moved around the woman's other side, she heard a whoosh and noticed water running down her leg. Her water had just broken.

Chapter Four

Chris had never been inside a maternity room before. He'd seen a lot of things in his twenty-eight years, including hard times and conditions not fit for any human being, but the inside of a birthing room had never been one of them.

The woman's name was Denise. She was in active labor and pushing as she squeezed his hand with a grip stronger than that of any guy he'd wrestled with. The doctor was there with two nurses and equipment. Everyone seemed to know their places and what they needed to do, everyone except him. He was in a hospital, holding the hand of a woman he'd known for less than three hours, having met her at a Starbucks after she'd accidentally grabbed his espresso instead of her hot chocolate. When she'd doubled over in labor, he could have walked away, but only scumbags did that, so instead he'd sat her down and driven her to the hospital. She'd told him her name and a little of her history, but labor had hit her hard and left her little time between contractions.

"Almost there, come on," said one of the nurses. "One more push, Denise."

She was a determined woman with dark hair, a round face, and lungs that rivaled her grip. The baby cried, and he was finally able to free his hand as all Denise's focus shifted to that small tiny bundle covered in blood. The nurse was wiping the baby clean. He heard it was a girl and wondered what the proper etiquette was for slipping out of a hospital room. He took a step back before a hand touched his arm.

"Did you bring a camera? Do you want me to take a photo of you and your wife with your new baby?" the nurse asked.

He glanced down at her, her dark hair hiked high in a ponytail. Her blue eyes had him taking a second look. "Sister of the bride, right? Trying to escape the flowers," he said. Of course, what was her name?

She actually winced. "A moment in time I'm doing my very best to forget. A ridiculous tradition to humiliate single women."

He realized she was waiting for something as he took her in. She gestured to Denise before clearing her throat, and he caught the meaning. "Her and I, we're not together," he said. "I just brought her to the hospital."

She actually raised an eyebrow and crossed her arms. Everyone was quiet, staring his way.

"Thank you again for driving me here," Denise said. She sounded tired, though for the first time since she'd doubled over, she was now able to string together a cohesive sentence without crying out in agony.

"Don't mention it. Glad I could help," Chris said. The bridesmaid was staring at him, and he wasn't sure what to make of her expression, so he held out his hand. "Chris MacDonald," he added.

She glanced at his hand for a second, leaving him thinking maybe she wouldn't take it. "Ivy Parker," she said, and then her hand was on his arm and she was walking him to the door. She pulled it open and stepped outside with him. "Can't say I've ever seen a perfect stranger in the delivery room before. A new one for me."

"I didn't know you worked at the hospital. You're a nurse?" What a stupid question. Of course she was. Small talk was something he never did.

"Yes," she said. Her hand was on the door, ready to dismiss him, and she was about to push it open.

"Wait."

She looked back to him. "Yes?"

"So this may sound kind of odd…"

"Ivy, sorry, excuse me," said a man from down the hall —a doctor, he presumed. He glanced to Chris and then Ivy. Chris could see his thinning dark hair and the way he gave all of his attention to Ivy, and Chris didn't move. Then the man rested his hand on her lower back, moving her a few steps farther away after saying, "Excuse us for a moment."

Her face and the man's expression had Chris realizing their conversation was personal, not professional, so he looked away, watching them from the corner of his eye.

"Was wondering if you're up for pizza, or we could just go to Tom's and have a burger and a pint?"

He could hear everything even though the man kept his voice low. Chris crossed his arms. So she was taken, but she'd said she was single. Just dating, maybe? The doctor rested his hand on her arm again, and he didn't miss the awkwardness from her.

"Sure, either is fine," she said, his arm still lingering with his thumb rubbing intimately. She seemed surprised, glancing back to Chris. New relationship, maybe? He stood there, his hand to his chin, thinking of his bags, which were packed in the trunk of his car. He'd already checked out of the hotel and had a long drive yet ahead.

The doctor was walking away, and Ivy was in front of him again. "So I never asked you," she said. "The wedding, you're a friend of Jerry's?" She was in pink and white scrubs, which were unflattering, but he really didn't notice the clothes. It was her, something about her.

"Yeah, we go way back, friends from school." He should go.

She held out her hand. "Well, Chris, it was nice to see you again—under unusual circumstances, I might add, but I need to get back. New mom, baby, you know." She gestured again to the door before pushing it open this time, and she glanced back to him once more before leaving him alone in the hallway.

He heard a woman scream from the room next door. It was definitely time to get out of there.

Chapter Five

The local bar two blocks away from the hospital was only half full as Ivy walked inside. The burgers were good, the beer was better, and the drunks were plentiful. Henry's hand was on her lower back again, which prompted her to move faster. He was nice, she liked him, but she was glad she'd insisted on driving her own car. He'd followed in his black Mercedes. Burger, beer, and then home.

"Not sure how good company I'm going to be," Ivy said. "I'm tired."

Her feet were still killing her as she slid into a booth, wearing blue jeans and a simple V-cut white sweater. She left her gray sweater coat over her shoulders and kept her hair pulled up in a ponytail. Her scrubs were in her bag in the backseat, waiting to be washed at home. Henry slid into the seat across from her, wearing a leather jacket over his white dress shirt and dark dress pants. He was soft in the middle, not something that had stood out before, but after seeing Chris, who was hard, chiseled, and badass, there was no comparison.

"Pint?" he asked her as a waitress appeared.

"Whatever's on tap," she said and nodded.

He held up two fingers. "And menus," he added before turning back to her, resting his arms on the table. The smile he had for her was nice. "So you live in Kaycee?"

Two mugs of draft appeared on the table, foam spilling over the tops. Henry slid one over to her.

"Thank you. Yes, I do, actually just outside the town. My father has a big place. I have a cottage on his property."

His eyes flashed with interest. She kept thinking of how nice Henry was, friendly. She'd always gotten along with him and had been out a few times with him and other hospital staff as a group, just never alone as they were now. This was a date, a real date.

"Has to be quite a commute every day," he said. "I have a house at the edge of Buffalo, good neighborhood. I bought it for the swimming pool. The old owner was another doctor who entertained a lot. Big for me, but always figured it'll be great when I settle down." He smiled her way again, and she lifted the mug to drink and wiped the foam she knew was on her lip. Sometimes she had to remind herself of the manners her mother had tried to instill in her.

"Sounds nice, so…" Good Lord, she totally sucked at small talk, even worse when she was tired.

"Did I hear right about a total stranger bringing a woman in and staying while she gave birth?"

"Hmm." She took another sip. "You did, a first. They met in a coffee shop, he said, and instead of calling 911, he brought her to the hospital. Thought he was with her. He was actually at my sister's wedding yesterday. Small world at times."

The waitress arrived. "Do you know what you'd like?"

Ivy hadn't even looked at the menu but knew it by heart. "Bacon cheeseburger with fries," she said and slid the menu to the side.

Henry flipped open his. "Make mine the chicken burger, side salad, though."

For a minute as she thought of her thighs, she felt guilty, as if she should have ordered the same. The waitress hurried away, and Henry was leaning on the table again, smiling, the light hitting his blue eyes. He was nice, kind, genuine, and would make a great husband—and he was interested in her. She felt nothing zinging between them, but they had a lot in common. Maybe.

"So you know the guy?" he said.

For a second, she had to stop and think who he was talking about. Then Chris's image hit her again: tall, ripped, a totally hunky bad boy who oozed chemistry and had her wishing she could see him again. What was his story?

"Not really. He was at the wedding. He's a friend of my sister's husband is all I know. Didn't know his name until tonight at the hospital, so I guess you could say I don't know him."

Then there was silence as Henry nodded and looked around, taking in the bar. "I wanted to ask you out for a long time but never knew whether you were really single or seeing anyone. You're not, right?"

Was he kidding? "Nope, not me. You?" she said, and he smiled again.

"Nope, just never met the right lady who held any interest to me, until now."

She hadn't expected that.

He held up his beer and took another swallow before

setting it down. "So tell me about you, Ivy Parker. Outside of work, what do you do? What interests you?"

What could she say? She worked, she went home, and she was surrounded by family, a close overprotective family. "What do you want to know about me? I have five sisters. Two are married, one up in Montana, Taz off on her honeymoon in Europe and living in Denver now, and that leaves just Naomi, who's a journalist, and Scarlett and Mason, the baby, who are both in high school. We have Sunday dinner and an overprotective father. There isn't much else. I'm not very interesting." She shrugged, because her fun downtime consisted of a hot bath, a good book, and a bowl of double chocolate fudge ice cream, which was likely the cause of her thick thighs and big ass.

"That's a lot, and you're wrong, Ivy. You are without a doubt the most fascinating woman I've ever met."

She was speechless. No man had ever said she was fascinating. "And what about you, Henry? You have family here?" Maybe kids, an ex, a past?

"Sure. Grew up in Buffalo but went to med school at UCLA. Met my wife there," he said. Maybe it was her expression that had him adding quickly, "Divorced a year later. Didn't last long. The residency of a young doctor is a relationship killer. No kids. Moved back here ten years ago now after I was offered a position in obstetrics I couldn't turn down. Took over as head of the department a year later, and the rest is history. Single doctor gives everything to a career, and now I've decided it's time settle down, to meet someone. Because of the crazy hours and dedication to this job, finding someone who understands the demands of a doctor and the fact that calls often come in the middle of the night is important. It takes a special kind of woman who can understand the job to make that relationship work." His gaze was intense and she understood his meaning. Henry Blackwell was very much interested in her.

When their burgers arrived, they chatted about the hospital, their cases, the staff, and nothing else personal. Work was an area far more comfortable for Ivy than more probing into her personal life, or his, or the idea that there could be something between them.

Chapter Six

C hris was at the end of the bar, coffee in hand, when he noticed Ivy sitting with the doctor from the hospital, laughing, chatting, and eating a burger. He'd never seen a woman dig in and enjoy a burger the way she did, but he could see the newly dating awkwardness and unease that oozed between the couple. Then he wondered, were they dating or was this just two colleagues having a drink and a bite? He'd bet his money on a date, first or second.

"Do you want another coffee or something else?" the bartender asked. The man was tall, large, and older, with an earring in one ear and shoulders that said he'd tossed out a drunk or two. He held up the steaming carafe of coffee.

"Sure, top it up," Chris said, and then what? Move on tonight or get another room? He was still deciding whether to drive through the night when he spotted Ivy and the doctor getting ready to leave. She said something to him, even touched his arm, and he pulled out his wallet and walked up to the bar as she walked to the back, down the hall to the restrooms.

"Thanks, Tom, just the bill please," the doctor said, and the bartender punched the register and printed out the bill.

"How goes the battle at the hospital, there, Doc?"

The doctor opened up his wallet, pulled out a wad of cash, and dumped it down. "Aw, you know, same old, pretty good. What can I say?"

"Did you and your lady friend there enjoy your burgers?"

Chris allowed the heat from the coffee mug to seep through his hands as he listened. This had to be a hangout for hospital staff.

"We did. It was either here or the pizza place. Just wasn't up for pizza tonight for a first date. You know Ivy's a nurse at the hospital. Finally got the nerve to ask her out," he said.

Chris was wondering why he'd say something like that, but he found people said the oddest things to bartenders. He glanced over to the restroom door.

"She's nice, young, not too old," the doctor said. "Never married and has family values, which doesn't hurt. Exactly the kind of woman I'm looking for. A little plump here and there, but she's got personality, which outweighs the fact that she couldn't pull off a bikini."

Chris couldn't believe the guy had said that. He found himself glancing back to the empty hallway again and wondering what Ivy had been thinking, going out with a guy like this. It was disrespectful that he was even talking about her size.

"But you also know what they say," the doctor continued. "Some of these big girls are wildcats in bed and will do things them skinny chicks won't."

The bartender laughed. Chris couldn't peel his eyes from the asshole doctor. Anything nice he'd thought about him had fled in that second. Not that Chris was a saint, but Jerry was his friend, and he was married to a nice girl. With Ivy being her sister, there was a family connection now. He wanted to have a word with this guy.

"There're gyms, too," he said. "I could get her to sign up for some classes and tone up. There are all kinds of possibilities." He actually tapped his fingers on the bar, and it wasn't lost on Chris that there was nothing buff about the guy. He doubted the man had spent any time lifting weights or working up a sweat. "But then, before things go much further, it's always best to test drive them, you know, make sure she can go the distance."

The two men actually laughed and bumped fists. Chris caught Ivy from his peripheral as she walked past them.

"Ready?" the doctor said to Ivy.

"Yeah. You didn't have to wait. I can walk to my own car."

"Of course not. What kind of guy would I be if I just left you here alone in a bar? Of course I'll walk you out. Wanted to ask you anyway about this Friday. I have the weekend off and was wondering if you'd like to come for dinner, my place?"

"Ivy." Chris couldn't stop himself from interrupting. Three pairs of eyes turned his way.

"Hey there, Chris. I didn't see you." She took a step closer and glanced back to the doctor, who was staring over at Chris, unsmiling. Of course he wasn't happy. Chris had just interrupted a play. The guy was working an angle, which shouldn't have bothered Chris, considering he himself had been with so many women he'd lost count and had never given most of them a second thought. He was ashamed that he'd probably said worse once or twice. Ivy was right in front of him, glancing to his coffee.

"Stopped for the coffee I missed earlier," Chris said. "You done your shift, on your way home?"

The doctor walked up behind her, close, and set his hand on her shoulder. She started. It was so subtle, and she glanced back but didn't move away. Chris recognized the proprietary gesture and the fact that Ivy appeared tired.

"Henry Blackwell." The doctor extended his hand around Ivy to Chris. "I work with Ivy."

Chris held out his large hand. The doctor's hand was soft, though the shake was firm, but not by much. "Chris MacDonald," he said.

"Chris is my sister's husband's friend, the one I was telling you about. He brought in the pregnant woman."

The doctor was grinning as if they had shared a private joke about him. "Oh yeah, swear that was a first at the hospital. Stranger in the delivery room. That was really cool of you to do that." Henry settled his hand on her arm again. Of course the move was to tell him to back off or something. He needed to go anyways. Forget the hotel—he'd drive through the night. He stepped down from the stool, pulled out his wallet, and tossed down a five for the coffee.

"It's what anyone would have done. I'll walk out with you," he said and started to the door.

Ivy reached it first, and he reached around her to pull it open for her and the doctor, who walked through. The night was dark, though the streetlights were lit. The parking lot beside the bar was mostly empty.

"So do you live in Buffalo?" Henry asked from the other side of Ivy, who was walking in between them. She was shorter and in sneakers, wearing a gray loose sweater over a light top.

"No, Kansas," he said and noted Ivy's glance his way.

"Didn't know that," she said. "Where are you staying?"

"Nowhere now. Checked out of my hotel and was just grabbing a coffee for the road before heading back home."

Ivy stopped, keys in hand, her blue eyes startled. "You're not seriously going to drive back tonight, are you?"

The doctor was staring at him now too.

"Of course," Chris said. "Not a big deal. Done it hundreds of times."

"Well, don't be silly," Ivy said. "It's late. You can stay in Taz's cabin. It's empty."

He noted the doctor's frown and just couldn't resist. "Sounds great," he said. "Why don't I follow you?"

Chapter Seven

She hadn't answered Henry about dinner on Friday. A date would be nice, but his place would be too intimate, and she wasn't sure she was up to it. Tomorrow she'd think about it. Tomorrow she would give him an answer.

She could see Chris in the rearview mirror driving his full-size pickup with mag wheels and tinted windows. The model was a few years old, the kind guys loved. She'd half expected to see a gun rack mounted in back, and maybe she still would in the light of day. She worried for a minute as she pulled down the darkened road to her parents' house, where the outside light was on. The flat thirty acres had been restored to its pre-wedding state. By the time she'd left for work late that morning, the last of the cleanup crew had been just leaving.

Ivy pulled her reliable Honda in front of Taz's empty cottage and parked. Chris pulled in beside her, and they both stepped out. She put her finger to her lips. "Shh, that's my parents' house. Dad's a light sleeper. Surprised he's not out here now."

He had to be tired. She knew the wedding had tired everyone out. She stepped up, her eyes adjusting to the dark. Chris shone his cell phone to light up the ground ahead of them.

"Nice place, cute. Your dad built these cabins? Jerry mentioned that." He was behind her as she popped open the front door and flicked the light on, taking in the neatness of the place even after Brandyne had stayed there the night before with her family.

"Yeah, Dad's protective. It's a long story," she finally said as she stepped inside. He let the screen close quietly. Smart man, she liked that, and so hot. She had to clear her throat. "I'll just check and see if the bed got made. My sister and her husband stayed here last night." She rested her purse on the table.

"The sheriff, Blake, right?"

She took in Chris, wondering how he knew.

"Jerry introduced me last night," he said. "Nice man. You have a nice family, too."

She wasn't sure what to say, considering Jerry hadn't introduced her to Chris or any of the male friends he'd invited. Now she had to wonder why. "So you live in Kansas," she said. "Do you have a family there?" She went to the stairs, hearing his footsteps behind her, following her up. He was alone here, so what was his story?

"Sure, cousins, and my mother," he said from behind her.

Just as she thought, the bed had been stripped. The duvet was folded, and the sheets were gone. She knew there would be more downstairs. "Let me get you some sheets and I'll make the bed for you."

She turned and bumped into him. He was so big, and she noticed his head just cleared the slope of the low loft ceiling. His hands gripped her arms.

"I can make a bed," he said. "You don't have to do that. You've already done a lot. This is nice. So this was Taz's place?" He was looking around, and she wasn't sure what it was she saw there as they stood beside the bed.

"Yeah—was, is. Not sure what will happen now. I know Scarlett would like to have it, but can't see Daddy or Mama letting her move in until she's out of high school."

He nodded again, and the way he was looking at her, she swore he could see through all her layers, straight through to what she hid from everyone. Knots twisted in her stomach as she felt mesmerized. She had to force herself to swallow as her heartbeat picked up, echoing. She wondered for a moment whether he could hear it.

Then he reached out, his fingers skimming her chin. They were rough and callused and felt so good. "You're so beautiful. Don't ever let anyone tell you anything less or try to fix you into their image of you."

She could feel her cheeks burn. Then he dropped his hand. She didn't know what that was about. "Okay," she said, fighting a wave of awkwardness. She reached for the rail and didn't think as she stepped down, twisting her foot. How, she had no clue, but her leg gave way and she felt herself falling.

Everything happened so fast as she tumbled down the stairs to the hard wood. Feet pounded behind her. She grabbed the railing halfway down, face first on her stomach, her ass in the air.

Yeah, totally awkward, embarrassing, and humiliating. He somehow had her sitting up and then was lifting her, carrying her down the stairs the rest of the way, sitting her in a chair before squatting down in front of her.

"Are you okay? Did you hurt yourself?" He was running his hands over her arms, down her legs, and he lifted her ankle and took her in, his gaze worried, intense.

"Ivy, answer me. Are you okay? That was a hard fall you took."

She moved her ankle and felt a twinge in her knee. She wasn't sure where she'd landed. "I'm fine, so sorry. That was such a klutzy, stupid move." She started to stand up, and he was wary, his hands out. She was fine, though her legs were a little shaky and her hip a little tight. She'd definitely be sore tomorrow and probably bruised in a few places—and she was embarrassed.

"Are you sure you're okay?"

"I'm fine, just stepped the wrong way. Let me get you those sheets and I'll make the bed for you." And then she would crawl back to her cabin. She could feel her knee now throbbing. She needed ice.

"Leave the sheets. Just point to where they are."

"Closet outside the bathroom, top shelf, should be a clean set. Okay, I'll leave you to it," she said and took a step, hobbling a bit. Next thing she knew, he'd lifted her in his arms. She squeaked, and he tossed her about to juggle her. "What are you doing?" She put her arms around his neck to hold on as he reached for the door.

"I'm carrying you back to your cabin," he said. He opened the door and stepped out, and a light flashed in her eyes.

"Care to explain what's going on?" It was her dad.

She lifted her hand to block the light, and Chris still had her in his arms. "I fell," she said. "Chris was just helping me back to my cabin. Dad, this is…"

"I know who it is. Chris MacDonald, right? You're a friend of Jerry's?"

Okay, so her dad knew more than she did.

Chris put her down, one arm still around her, and held out his hand to her dad. "Great to see you again, Mr.

Parker. Your daughter offered to let me stay here tonight instead of driving back to Kansas."

Her dad said nothing, and she wasn't in a mood to explain. "Long story, Dad. Didn't think you'd mind him staying the night at Taz's."

Awkward, considering Chris still had one arm around her, holding her up, and her dad hadn't missed that.

"You fell?" he said. "You okay, Ivy? Should I get your mother?"

That was the last thing she needed, for her mom to be out here too. "No, Dad, don't wake up Mom. Just going to put ice on my knee and then go to sleep."

Then her father did something she'd never have expected. He shone the light at the ground and stepped down. "Okay, then. Good night, you two. Chris, come over for breakfast in the morning."

Then he walked away, and Chris lifted her once again in his arms. She could feel his muscles tighten and the easy way he moved in the dark, carrying her as if she weighed nothing.

Chapter Eight

C hris had showered and changed into fresh clothes from the bag in his truck after carrying Ivy to the cabin behind Taz's. It wasn't lost on him when he set her down in the kitchen chair that the cabins were identical. He'd pulled ice from the freezer, packed it in a Ziploc bag, and wrapped a dishtowel around it. Ivy had taken the ice pack, rested it on her knee, and assured him she was fine.

He'd waited outside her cabin for a time, though, until he saw the lights go on and off upstairs. Then he returned to Taz's cabin, rustled up some sheets, and made the bed. He'd been asleep by the time his head had hit the pillow, and he didn't wake until he heard voices outside. The sun was up, and the clock was flashing just past eight. Now, as he strode across the yard to Taz's parents' place, where the front door was open, he took in Ivy's cabin, which was quiet. He was tempted to check on her, but at the same time he didn't want to wake her.

The screen door opened by the time his booted foot hit the first step. The younger sister who greeted him, a dark-haired beauty, had a killer smile and a body to go along with it. She was dressed in cutoffs and a rust-colored tank top that was loose and showed her bra underneath. "Hey there, Chris," she said. "Daddy said Ivy put you up last night at our sister's. Great to see you again." She was flirting with him and even batted her lashes. He knew it came naturally to some women—and some teens.

"And you are?" He couldn't remember her name.

She pressed her hand to her chest, taking a step closer to him and eyeing him up. "Scarlett. Well, come on in. There's coffee on." She looped her hand through his arm after they stepped inside and linked her other around it, holding on to him and pressing close to him. He could feel the sway in her hips, all sex, no sense. Trouble, she was. "I made the biscuits this morning, and I can whip you up some eggs, and there's a wad of bacon, too, in the fridge. Could fry it up for you," she said.

He wanted to disengage her from his arm as he took in Robert and Susan Parker in the kitchen. Another sister with bright hair that was a cross between pink and red was spooning cereal into her mouth. She lifted her hand. "You must be Chris," she said. Milk spilled out of her mouth, and she wiped at it.

"Don't talk with your mouth full, Mason, and use a napkin," Susan said. "Scarlett, let go of that man and get on in here and unload the dishwasher. Chris, coffee's on. Help yourself." She pulled a mug from the cupboard and set it down in front of a full coffeepot.

"Thank you," he said as he poured a cup, but he didn't clarify that his thanks was more for their help in peeling their daughter away from him than for the coffee.

"Milk and sugar is on the table already," Susan said. "How about some eggs? Two, three?" she asked, taking him in.

He took a seat at the table. Robert Parker was at the head, and Mason was across. "Sure, two would be great."

Biscuits filled a bowl, and there was a jar of jam and a small plate with butter. Susan set a plate with two biscuits in front of him while he added sugar to his coffee and stirred with one of the four spoons piled in the center of the table.

"Thank you," he said.

Susan was in capris and a blue shirt, sleeveless and buttoned up the front. She had a great figure, and Robert was watching him and not saying a word. The screen door squeaked, and he turned to see another sister, with glasses and dark hair so long it went past her butt. She was in ripped jeans and a baggy T-shirt, sandals on her feet. She stumbled when she saw Chris. He nodded.

"Naomi, this is Chris, a friend of Jerry's. He stayed in Taz's place last night," Scarlett said as she bounced over to her sister and put an arm around her.

"Chris, nice to meet you." Naomi was still looking at him as she went to the coffeepot, filled a mug, and sat down at the table beside Mason, who was now reaching for a biscuit. Crumbs flew everywhere as she took a big bite.

"You too," Chris replied.

"Okay, here you are. Two eggs over easy. Hope that's how you like them." Susan was carrying a frypan and scooped two eggs onto the plate in front of him.

"Thank you. This looks great, and I appreciate the hospitality."

Then he heard a car start, and Scarlett called out, "That's Ivy leaving. Guess she has the early shift."

"Mind your business, Scarlett, and finish the dishwasher," Susan said. "Your sister has a busy career. Didn't she work late last night, and now early this morning? She's not getting much down time." She walked to the window, and

Chris turned toward it. He could see for miles outside, including Ivy's car and a trail of dust behind it. He wanted to thank her, to check on her and see whether she was okay, but he needed to get home, too, back to Kansas City, which was hours from here.

When he looked back around, he noticed the sisters each watching him with interest, curiosity, and something else from Scarlett. That one, he swore, was walking trouble and left him feeling a little uneasy. Maybe it would be best to finish, pack up, and leave Ivy a note instead. That would be the smartest play for sure.

Chapter Nine

Four hours into her double shift, Ivy was resting behind the nurses' station with a double espresso and a sore knee, which had been bruised but thankfully not swollen this morning when she woke. Her ankle felt as if she'd wrenched it, so instead of racing around the floor as she normally did, she was doing her feet and knee a favor and resting them as much as she could. Thankfully, the day shift in the maternity ward was relatively quiet. It was often nights when the craziness began. What was it about babies that they could never wait until a reasonable hour to arrive?

"Hey, there. I didn't know you were working early today," Henry said. He was in a deep blue golf shirt, looking well rested.

"Wasn't supposed to be, but I got called in. They were short staffed. Apparently a flu is going around, so lucky me is doing a double," she added before lifting her coffee and taking a swallow, wishing the caffeine buzz would kick in and lift the cobwebs from her head. She wanted a nap. She wanted to lay her head down for just five minutes.

"You couldn't have gotten much sleep." He made a face.

"Not bad. Five hours, give or take. Have had less, and so have you." She gestured to him and then put her coffee down. "I just need to wake up and then I'll be fine."

"Well, how about I take you for lunch at the cafeteria?"

"Don't know when I can get away," she said as he leaned on the counter.

"You just page me when you're ready and I'll slip away. So did you get that friend of your brother-in-law's all squared away?"

"Ah, Chris?" She'd pulled away that morning in such a hurry, and she was kicking herself now for having been such a big chicken. She'd known he was at her parents', most likely being fed, and instead of going in and saying goodbye, she'd been so embarrassed still at her ungraceful fall on the stairs that she'd wanted to slink away and hide. Now she wished she could go back and have a do over, but it was too late. He'd be another state away, and she'd likely never see him again. "I'm sure he's halfway back to Kansas now, but thanks for asking."

What was it she saw in his expression right before he smiled? "So, Friday. You didn't tell me if you're free."

No, she hadn't answered him. "I'm off Thursday, Friday, and Saturday so far unless I'm called in," she said.

"Great. Well, how about dinner my place on Friday? I make a mean paella." He was leaning closer, and she was trying to picture what being with a man like Henry would be like. He was respected, attentive. He was the perfect catch, right?

"Sounds great. Would love that." She smiled, and he tapped the counter.

"Great. I'll text you my address."

Then he was pulled away to deal with a laboring mom, and the desk phone rang.

"Maternity," she said, wondering whether the peace and quiet was about to end.

"I have a visitor downstairs for Ivy Parker," the receptionist said on the other end.

"This is Ivy. Who's there?"

She heard talking in the background, a man's voice. "He says his name is Chris MacDonald."

Why was he here? "Okay, I'll be right down," she said before setting the phone back in the cradle. "Jody, can you watch the desk? I'm going to take my coffee break right now."

Jody was the head nurse, tall, male, and African American, with skin so dark it was almost black. He wandered over behind the desk with a chart. "For sure. Good time to take it while it's slow. Hey, can you bring me back a coffee with cream, two sugars?"

"You got it," she said as she slipped into the back and grabbed her purse from her cubby. Then she was buzzed out of the locked ward.

She spotted Chris as soon as she stepped off the elevator. He wasn't the kind of man who could fade into any background. He was in blue jeans and a short-sleeved shirt that showed his extremely impressive arms. No wonder he'd had little trouble lifting her weight. She had to look up as she approached him, and his amazing smile instantly increased her heart rate. How did he do that, and why was she so affected by him?

"I thought you were heading back to Kansas?" she said, holding her purse strap in one hand.

"I was, but it didn't seem right to leave without thanking you and checking to see how you are, which appears to be fine." He gestured toward her knee.

"Sorry, I just have a few bruises. I've had worse, not a big deal. It was more my pride was injured, is all. You realize you're kind of going out of your way?" She couldn't remember any man ever having gone to this much effort.

"Not really. Your hospitality was welcome. Met all your family this morning and was fed by your mom," he said. She could just imagine him being swarmed by everyone. She was glad now she had left. At times they could be smothering.

"Well, you appear to have escaped unscathed. Bring us all together in a room, me and my sisters. Just ask Jerry what an experience that is."

His smile turned to laughter, and she could see he'd experienced something. Scarlett, most likely, at her finest, with Naomi questioning him and Mason pouring on all her charm. She wanted to ask but thought better of it.

"It was nice to see a family unit so close," he said. "You have a great family. You have time for coffee?" He gestured to the hallway that led to the cafeteria.

"I do, but do you mind if we go outside? There's a coffee cart, and I'd just as soon get out in the fresh air, since I'm going to be cooped up here for a double."

He was watching her as they walked out the front doors, people passing them in and out. It was a busy place. "That sounds like a long day," he said.

"Sixteen hours." She sighed. "But after that I just have tomorrow, and then I have three days off. I'm so looking forward to it."

"You must enjoy what you do," he said as they fell in behind a man wearing surgical scrubs paying for a coffee at the outside kiosk.

"I do. I've always wanted to be a nurse. You could say it was my calling."

He was smiling at her again. "So what does Ivy Parker do for fun on her three days off?" He sounded as if he was teasing her, and she wondered what he'd say.

"Not much. Read lots, get pestered by my sisters. Sometimes I'll drive to Buffalo to meet friends for a movie, or here in Kaycee. It's a quiet life." And she had a date this weekend, which she was still trying to wrap her head around. No one asked her out ever, and the male attention as of late was having her take a second look in the mirror. "Dinner out Friday," she said. Now why had she shared that?

He was looking down at her again. "Sounds fun, a date?" he asked.

She looked up to him as they walked. She could feel her hip and knee loosening. It felt good to move. "Yeah, as a matter of fact, it is."

"That doctor guy you were with last night?"

"Henry? Yes." It felt odd talking about him with Chris. They were both so different.

"You been seeing him long?"

Personal and intrusive. Why exactly was he interested?

"No. We went out last night after work, first time. Didn't think he was interested in me. How about you? Dating anyone?" She couldn't believe she'd asked that.

He smiled again. "Nope."

"Well, what about work? What exactly do you do in Kansas?"

"Work for myself. Started out in metal manufacturing, parts and stuff for contractors, and kind of expanded from there. I have other contracts, retail and stuff, and I can tell by the way you're looking at me that you have no idea what I'm talking about."

She didn't have a clue, really. Her dad was the builder

and worked with everything mechanical. He'd probably understand more of what Chris did than she ever could. Anything to do with that kind of thing made her eyes glass over. It sounded boring. "Not my thing, sorry. That's why I'm a nurse," she added.

He ordered two coffees, handed one to her, and shook his head when she tried to pay. "No, I got this," he said. Then he was dumping sugar into his paper cup, and Ivy slid a sleeve over hers so she wouldn't burn her fingers.

They were walking again. He sipped on his coffee and gestured to an empty park bench. She sat down, and he took a seat beside her, leaning forward, his arms resting on his knees as he dangled his coffee in one hand between his legs. His back was impressive, and she had to fight the urge to touch him, to reach over and feel the strength she knew had to ooze from it.

She spotted some ink on the side of his arm, just the edge of a tattoo that had to be just below his shoulder. She wondered what it was. Maybe he noticed her looking at it, as he pulled at the edge of his shirt to hide it.

"Sorry, I didn't mean to stare."

He shrugged. "It's fine, just a tattoo. Don't show it often."

"Why? I happen to like tattoos. Is it a girl's name? Please tell me you didn't have a girl's name tattooed on your arm, and now you've broken up and it's there as a permanent reminder of a moment in time you wish you could go back and change."

He started laughing, and it was even better than his voice. He shook his head. "Quite the imagination you have. I'm sure lots of guys have found themselves in that predicament and done something that stupid, but no." He lifted his sleeve, and she was stunned by the artwork. It was a chopper and what looked like three soldiers below with guns in a field.

"Wow, that's gorgeous." She wanted to run her fingers over the colors, the green, the red, the blue, the detail, and at the same time she took in something about him that seemed so serious. She could feel him tense as if he knew she was about to touch him, so she pulled her fingers back, rested them around her hot cup of coffee.

He dropped his sleeve and leaned back, gazing out into the distance.

"Were you in the military?"

"Army," he said and then nothing else. She wondered what had happened that had him shutting down. He still hadn't looked at her but was scanning the people, back and forth. When he glanced her way again, there was a sadness there that hadn't been before.

"How long?" she asked, and he flicked his gaze away again.

"Long enough. Enlisted when I was eighteen and was out three years ago. Took two of them to pull my shit together." He glanced her way again.

"What made you choose the army?" She wasn't opposed to it, but she'd seen too many fucked-up soldiers come back. Some handled it well, many didn't.

He shrugged. "Wasn't a choice, really. Grew up in a part of Kansas where you aren't left with many choices. You either join the military or you end up in jail. The only sure thing in the community I grew up in was the poverty that breeds there. Only a few find a way to a scholarship and pull themselves up from nothing. Being poor still doesn't leave you many options," he added, and she said nothing. She'd grown up poor, but unlike many, she knew her family had love.

Then he stood up and dumped his half-drank coffee in

the trash. It was humbling and sad, because she realized he was leaving. He looked down at her and all her frumpiness, and she couldn't make out what she saw there.

"Be careful with Henry Blackwell," he said. "He may not be who you think he is."

Then he lifted his hand and left, leaving her to wonder what the hell he meant by that.

Chapter Ten

Chris had made good time, eleven hours and sixteen minutes, on the drive from Buffalo to his home just outside Kansas City. It wasn't a large house, just an average affordable bungalow at the edge of a relatively rough area that bordered an up and coming suburbia.

He lifted his bag from the back of his pickup and unlocked his door, taking in the dark. When he flicked on his light, he saw his black cat, Tuffy, curled up in an easy chair. She lifted her head and meowed before jumping down and demanding his attention.

"Well, you look like you had tons of fun. Quite the life, there." He scratched her neck until she'd had enough and then stretched before walking into the kitchen to the dog dish he kept overfilled. The cat did what she always did and then slipped through the cat door and outside. He took in his small galley kitchen and the light blinking on his phone.

He played the messages, first a wrong number, then a telemarketer for some upscale resort. He deleted both and dropped his keys, then pulled his wallet from his back pocket and threw that on the small kitchen table. He took in the sparsely furnished place. It was perfect for him and all he needed, but it was a far cry from the homey feel of the Parkers' place.

He wondered how Ivy was. She'd likely still be at work, or maybe almost done. He was tired, but she had to be exhausted.

"Not for you. Get her out of your head," Chris reminded himself as he sat down at his computer at a small table in the living room. He pulled up the emails he hadn't checked since leaving for Jerry's wedding three days before, and he spotted an email from the man himself. He clicked it open, wondering why a man on his honeymoon was emailing anyone, let alone him.

Just checking you made it back. Thanks for coming. Taz mentioned an email from home that you stayed the night. What gives? My wife wants some answers.

He leaned back in his chair and wondered which one of her sisters was stirring up trouble. So it was Taz who couldn't stay off the computer and away from family.

He pulled up the email and hit reply. *Nothing to worry about, long story. Will share when you get back. Ran into her, it was late, she offered me a place.* He stopped typing, looking at the message. He was still bothered by the comments of that doctor. Why, he didn't know. It wasn't as if he hadn't done that same thing and so much worse, but there was something about Ivy and their new family connection that came with a conscience, so he started typing again. *Just a heads up, too, the guy she's dating may be a douchebag. He isn't a great guy. Warned her off, but not sure if she got it.*

Then he hit send. There, conscience cleared. Now he could get back to…what, exactly?

His cell phone started ringing. He pulled it from his

pocket and couldn't believe he saw Jerry's number. "Why are you calling me on your honeymoon?"

"I just got your message, was online. Please tell me what this is about, because if I share what you just emailed with my wife, she'll lose it. Are you telling me some guy is messing with Taz's sister?"

Why had he emailed that? Seriously, what was wrong with him?

"Overheard this doctor guy she was with—first date, I think—going on to the bartender about her. He's not dating her for her mind. She may think his intentions are honorable, but the guy's a scumbag. Hey, listen. I don't really know Ivy, but she seems nice and she offered me a place so I didn't have to drive all night. I didn't like the way he was talking about her. It was uncool."

"You're being cryptic, and I don't like cryptic. You do know that Taz's parents, her father, won't stand for someone messing with his daughter."

He'd gotten that from the man, yeah, and he'd also gotten that Ivy didn't really know this doctor guy as well as she thought. "Look, if it were anyone else, I wouldn't say anything. I'd say she's a big girl, she can figure it out, but there's a line of respect. Maybe we've all crossed that with women and never given it a second thought. I didn't really get it until now."

There was silence on the other end. "So is this just some creep looking for sex, or do you have a thing for Ivy?"

Chris pulled the phone away and stared at it. "You know what? Never mind, forget I said anything. Go back to your honeymoon." He disconnected the phone, still shaking his head, when his email dinged and a message appeared in his inbox from Jerry. He clicked it open.

Don't mess with Ivy, because Taz will kill me, and then I'll have to hurt you. And P.S., give me the name of the scumbag who's messing with her. I'll see to it that he leaves her alone.

Instead of emailing back, Chris closed down his computer and walked into the kitchen to figure out what to eat, but all that stared back at him were empty cupboards, freezer-burned steak, and stale bread in the fridge.

Chapter Eleven

Her phone was ringing as she climbed out of the bathtub, wrapped a large bath sheet around herself, and ran to the living room.

"Good morning," she said, praying it wasn't work, because there was no way she was giving up one day of her three-day weekend. She was exhausted from two double shifts back to back and had literally crawled into bed the night before when she got home.

"Hey."

It was his voice that got her, and it took a second for her to understand this wasn't a mind fuck. It really was him calling. "Chris?" she said, holding the towel together in front, seeing the sun spill in the windows.

"In the flesh—well, over the phone, that is. Just called to see how you're doing?" He sounded happy and something else. Seriously, now why would mister tall and drop-dead gorgeous be calling her anyway? She hadn't even give him her phone number.

"I'm good. How are you? How was your drive back to Kansas?" This was so weird.

"Fine. It was no big deal, just another drive. So…"

Then there was awkwardness.

"Chris, what's going on? And, by the way, how did you get my number, anyway? I don't remember giving it to you." She walked into the living room, the water dripping down her legs. She sat in the easy chair, crossing legs that were far from slender. To her they were starting to resemble tree trunks. She needed to do something about the weight that seemed to be piling on her, widening her ass and her thighs.

"Jerry sent me your number. He got it from Taz."

"They're supposed to be on their honeymoon, not talking to people. Did you call him for my number?" This was really getting weird, and why were Taz and Jerry giving her number to Chris?

"No, I didn't. Apparently one of your sisters has been emailing Taz and mentioned me staying there. I arrived home to an email from Jerry wanting to know what was up. Long story short, he emailed your phone number to me."

She knew who the instigator was. Scarlett, it had to have been. The little shit was always stirring something up. But bugging Taz on her honeymoon was seriously crossing a line. Ivy had every intention of going over and having a talk with her when she got home from school. "Sorry about that." She was mortified.

"No worries. That wasn't the only reason, though." He said nothing else, and she couldn't help thinking of the two different personalities she'd seen from Chris. He was a complex man with a past, and maybe a lot of it was something he didn't want to share.

"What else is there?"

"I wanted to ask you out," he said.

She pulled the phone away and stared at it again

before putting it back to her ear. This was crazy, two men, all of a sudden, out of the blue, interested in Ivy Parker, the one sister who couldn't turn a man's eye. "You want to ask me out on a date? You live in Kansas, which is, what, twelve, thirteen hours away?"

"Eleven and a bit—and yes, for dinner."

"You want to take me out to dinner? Where?" This was crazy.

"There, in Kaycee," he said, sounding as if it were completely logical for him to get in his truck and drive eleven hours. It was a frickin' big deal, and totally crazy.

"So you're planning on driving eleven hours and change to Kaycee to take me for dinner?"

"Yes," he said, sounding certain.

"Okay, when?" She was ready to humor him, thinking that maybe this was some joke and he was about to tell her the punchline.

"Tonight," he said, and she realized he was serious. Her towel slipped, her stomach knotted, and her mouth suddenly became dry. She had to clear her throat.

When she opened it, all that came out was "Sure."

Chapter Twelve

I t was just after six when Chris parked in front of the main house. Sitting on the porch were Robert and Susan Parker, who waved when he pulled up. Mason came around the side, carrying a bucket, with two dogs he hadn't seen before following her.

He closed the door of his truck and stepped up the first step. Scarlett burst out of the house, wearing a red sleeveless blouse and a short skirt. She stopped and reached for the rail, then leaned against it provocatively.

"Scarlett, did you finish peeling the potatoes?" her mother asked.

"All done. So you drove all this way out here to see Ivy?" The way she said it sounded so mean spirited.

"Yes, I did," he said and looked over to Robert Parker, who was staring at his daughter as if he couldn't believe what had come out of her mouth. "Is Ivy in her cabin?" he asked.

One of the dogs, a large mixed mutt, wandered over, its tail wagging and wanting a pet. He leaned down and rubbed behind the dog's ears.

"Ivy is getting ready. She's changed three times already," Mason said from where she stood beside him. She had gumboots on as if she'd been walking in mud, and her hair was no longer an odd shade of red, now golden with a hint of orange. "She's excited, though. So you're a friend of Jerry's?" She was eyeing him up, not the way Scarlett had, more like she was protective of Ivy. He was starting to wonder about these Parker sisters.

"Go on over. Where are you planning on going for dinner?" Susan asked.

"Well, didn't get that far yet but hoped Ivy had some ideas for places in town, or can you recommend someplace good?"

"Well, you can stay for dinner here," Susan suggested. Robert Parker settled his hand over hers and squeezed.

"He drove all this way to take Ivy out. Try that new steak place in town. Heard it's pretty good."

"The pub, too. They have such great burgers, and we all know how much Ivy loves her burgers." Scarlett literally ran her hand over her ass. It was cruel, the insinuation.

"Scarlett, that's enough," her father reprimanded.

Her expression was sullen as if she were the one who'd been wronged. "Just saying we've all noticed all the weight she's put on. You even said so."

"You're mean, Scarlett," Mason blurted out, and for a moment it seemed as if the girls were going to hash it out.

"Scarlett, go pull the laundry from the washer and hang it out on the line while the sun's still out. Mason, those dogs aren't coming in unless you get them bathed," Susan said.

Chris took that as his cue to step down and start over to Ivy's cottage.

He knocked on her door and heard footsteps. Then the door opened and he took her in. Her dark hair was straight and long, brushed straight to her midback, and she was wearing makeup and eyeshadow. He couldn't get over how the blueness in her eyes really popped. She was in black capris and a silky brown and black top with lacy straps.

She smiled. "I can't believe you were serious about driving all the way back here to take me out to dinner." She stepped back and then peeked out. "Where's your truck?" She closed the door.

"In front of your parents' place. Figured it was the right thing to do, considering they were sitting out there, waiting."

She nodded. "Smart. Let me just get my shoes, and we can go." She darted up her stairs, and he still couldn't get the image of her tumbling down the identical set next door out of his head. She seemed okay, though. "So I wanted to ask," she called out from the loft. "You aren't planning on driving all the way back to Kansas after dinner, are you?" She came back carrying a pair of sandals with a slight heel, and she held the rail on her way down the stairs.

"No, I'm going to grab a room at the motel in town." He hadn't reserved one but was pretty sure it wouldn't be a problem. Worst case, he'd drive to Buffalo.

"Don't be silly. You can stay at Taz's. Guess I can't keep calling it Taz's place for much longer, considering she doesn't live there anymore." She slipped her feet into the sandals and picked up a purse on the table. Then she was looking up at him, and the expression on her face suddenly turned serious. "Can I ask you something, Chris?" She was holding the chair. Her fingers gripped the edge.

"Of course you can." He stepped closer to her.

"What is it you really want from me?" she said. The expression on her face had turned sad, worried. That was definitely not what he'd been expecting.

Chapter Thirteen

He gave nothing away as he stood before her in the middle of her kitchen, just ten feet from her front door. He didn't shove his hands in his faded blue jeans pockets or fidget as some guys did when put under the spotlight. Instead he crossed his arms, his sleeves rolled up, his flexed forearms pulling at the seams of his off-white dress shirt. But she was far from a weak woman who'd cave to a man, no matter how hot he was.

"Where is this coming from?" he asked.

She hated that shit. "You're asking a question from a question, seriously? Just answer me straight out, and be honest: What is this? Because have you looked at yourself in the mirror and then looked at me?" She swallowed the building ache in her throat, knowing she wasn't a beauty queen and dimmed in comparison to all of her sisters. She knew that, accepted that, and wondered now what this was. The longing was so great that she knew she'd be crushed if she allowed this fantasy to go on one second more. *Please don't lie to me!*

"You really think I have some agenda, driving

hundreds of miles, hours, to see you, be with you, and you're thinking…?" He was shaking his head, his expression so intense, digging in and stripping her down as if trying to find that secret place where she was determined to protect all of herself—but that place was something she just couldn't hand over to him.

She shrugged. She was stuck on the seeds of doubt that had been planted.

"Is this just you wondering because you think you're less in some way, or is someone messing with your head?" he asked, shrewdness building in the way he focused on her.

She had to look away. The doubts had nipped at her when she woke early that morning and throughout the day in moments when she wasn't thinking or neck deep in work, doubts that had grown over the years from passing comments. "I know I'm not a toothpick or one of those skinny girls you guys like," she said, crossing her arms over the ache now building in her stomach.

"Who put that in your head?" he demanded, coming at her now, strong and forceful. "Your sister, someone else?" He really studied her, and she wanted to believe he was the good guy and really did want her for herself, but that was a fantasy she couldn't allow herself to believe.

"Okay, yes. My bratty younger sister has pointed out so many times that I'm limited in my choice of men, and so has Henry. I mentioned in passing that you were driving back to take me out, and he let me know that guys like you have agendas, intentions other than dating me or building something with me—as if you'd expect me to be the kind of girl you wouldn't take home to your mother. Do I need to spell it out to you graphically that he thinks this is about power and control, not respect?" She could feel her cheeks burning. She couldn't get out the words he'd actually used:

sex, domination, things beyond anything she was comfortable with. Then he'd dump her when he was finished. It was cruel and it hurt, and she was still trying to shake it off.

"Are you fucking kidding me? That prick said that to you?" He leaned in, and she could tell how pissed he was. "And you believed him?"

She didn't know what to say and didn't know Chris well enough to know whether he was being honest or furious at having been called out.

"Answer me, then," she said. "I'm a person. I have feelings, I hurt, I bleed, I cry just like everyone else." She was unsure of what to do with her hands. She was uncomfortable and didn't know how to resolve this situation.

"Of course you do, I know that, but what you don't know is that those words he told you are exactly what he himself said. I know this sounds ridiculous, but you have to know that Henry Blackwell is messing with you. What he told you were his words, his thoughts, his plans. He's not trying to protect you. He has an agenda with you." Chris was pacing, furious, clenching his fists like a caged animal. The room had gone suddenly cold with tension. "You said he told you all this, and I bet he also tried to convince you to cancel plans with me and instead go out with him?"

"No, he didn't, but he did tell me that he cared about me and my feelings and that you've done this before. He said that as my friend, he needed to explain to me the monster that lives in all men, and it all stems from their need to gain as much power and control as they can. It's natural for them to try to steal it away from someone weaker. That's why they steal it from women. I've witnessed this, heard it in the hospital dozens of times. I just never expected a colleague to have to sit me down and explain your plan to maneuver me into a position where I depend on you for everything. I know how the cycle works:

Beat the woman down and break her skillfully to deny her the right to make decisions. Make all her decisions for her and direct her life, telling her how to think, feel, do. All just to increase your sense of significance and status, to offset your discontent and sense of unworthiness because society has changed the rules and balanced the rights—"

"Stop it!" he yelled and took a step. His hands were fisted, and she could see the color in his face. "You really think I could be that kind of man? Yeah, you bet I understand all of that. Every man does. For centuries men had all the power, and women didn't. But you have that all fucked up and backwards, that bullshit psychological analysis. I want you because of who you are and this light that shines in you—and yeah, some guys get off on a need to be better, to have it all, to make everyone believe what they believe, but making me into that... No!" He pointed forcefully. "Let me tell you that the guys who do that are the ones who've never learned that they have everything they need. They're the ones who believe the only way they can be better is to make someone else less. They're the guys who are in the shadows of everything. They need to prop up their egos, their senses of self-worth, at the expense of making another person weaker, and yes, that person often is a woman. But that's not me. I want to get to know you for you."

This was so confusing. Was Henry wrong? "So why did Henry say all that to me? I know him, worked for years with him. Can you honestly tell me you've never treated a woman as if she were nothing but a sex toy for you, some plaything you could toss away when you were done and you got what you needed, and your expectation of her was to be nothing, no one, but to do what you said and then just go away because you were done with her?"

He was quiet now, and her heart sank a little. "I never

said I was a saint, Ivy. I have a past I'm not proud of and have done things with women that weren't okay, but I guarantee you I've never tried to break a woman, not like that, or have her be my puppet. I've screwed a lot of faceless women and probably said whatever I needed to get them on their backs, no strings, no commitments. But what you're talking about is something that takes time, and it's not the same. It's cold and calculating. And a person who does that is someone who doesn't respect women or anyone."

Maybe, or maybe he wanted her to believe what he was saying. Was this just another way to work her? She touched her fingers to her head when he stepped closer still.

He gestured to the floor. "This here is me taking the time to get to know you, not tell you how to think, feel." He became so quiet, stepping closer to her, his hand on her arm, slipping around her back and holding her. "And so you know, men are dogs until they find the one."

Then he leaned in, his face close to hers, his eyes wide open as he pressed a kiss to her, her hand touching his chest, feeling his heart, the beat and tension and every hard thing about him. When he pulled back, the intimacy and rawness of the moment answered nothing and every-thing at once.

Chapter Fourteen

He was staring up at the ceiling, the early morning light sifting through the window. He'd fallen asleep and had woken with his mind racing, unable to get past that fucker Henry Blackwell and how he'd twisted his interest in Ivy. He knew what the guy was doing, eliminating the competition by taking him out and easing Ivy over to his camp, beginning phase one of controlling her. The guy was good, and Chris had never expected that kind of turnabout.

Of course, he hadn't told Ivy what he'd overheard in the bar. Henry had no respect for her, and it had sickened him to hear him bragging about his plans to change her, control her. She had no idea who she was dealing with, seeing he had everything on his side. He wasn't handsome, but he had a great career and was already friends, so to speak, with her. He had her ear and came off as someone who could offer her far more than any other man. Chris wondered how many women he'd broken.

He rubbed his head, pushing back the duvet of Taz's bed and slipping out naked. He pulled on jeans before making his way down the stairs to the shower. Yes, he'd taken Ivy for dinner. She'd opted for a burger, and so had he. They'd chatted about anything but the albatross that hung heavy in the room, and neither mentioned the kiss. It had shaken him, and at the same time he'd seen how rattled she'd become. It had scared her, too, and he suspected that was her fear of allowing anyone in. As he stood in the hot shower, he reminded himself not to push, to take baby steps with Ivy, but at the same time he needed her to believe he'd never hurt her, not like that.

By the time he'd dressed in clean clothes and stepped outside, he noted that Robert Parker was just loading up his rusty old truck with tools and such. He didn't say a word as he walked over, and Robert closed up the back.

"So, didn't hear you two come back last night. Where did you and Ivy end up?"

"The new steak place." He gestured with his thumb to Taz's cabin. "Thanks again for the place to stay."

Robert Parker didn't smile but glanced over to Ivy's place. "Ivy's up."

Chris turned to see her walking his way, her hair pulled back in a ponytail, wearing a baggy T-shirt and blue jeans. She lifted her hand in the air and said, "Good morning." He supposed that was for both him and her father. "Hey there," she said to him when she reached them. Her smile was distant.

"So what are you two up to today?" Robert asked.

"Well, I'm sure Chris has to get back to Kansas. Wasn't sure how early you planned to leave, so I thought we could have coffee. I can make you breakfast," she added, linking her fingers together, still nervous.

"You know what? Breakfast and coffee would be great. Thought I'd stick around another day, though, if that's all right. Maybe we could catch a movie tonight in Buffalo?"

She cocked her head, her arms crossed. "Can do breakfast, but I already told you I have plans tonight," she said. "Daddy, where you off to?"

He couldn't remember ever having been dismissed in such a way.

"Got some more work at the oilfield, repairs that should keep me busy the next few weeks. Chris, stick around as long as you want. We have the room," Robert said before focusing his attention on his daughter. "Where you off to tonight, then?"

"Just dinner plans I made with Dr. Blackwell earlier in the week." She lifted her chin as she said it, and he could see nothing but stubbornness.

No one said anything as her father walked around the truck and pulled open the door. "See you later, then. Chris, you're welcome to join us for dinner," he added, but he didn't wait for his reply as he climbed in and started the old truck, which purred loudly. Then he pulled away.

"You're still going to his place for dinner?" Chris said.

She shrugged. "Of course I am. I committed earlier in the week."

"So this is about commitment, then?" He could see her thinking.

"Yes…no. Look, I don't know, but I do know I want to go for dinner with him. We've worked together for a lot of years, and I'm not committed to him or you," she said.

He took in Scarlett and Mason stepping out on the front porch and watching them. "Look, even after last night, you and I…"

She was waving her hands. "No, whoa, just stop. There is no you and I. You drove out here, took me for dinner, kissed me, and then what?" She was shaking her head. "We're not committed to each other. I still don't know what this is." She was rattled, and he could hear in her voice that she still didn't believe it was about her.

How was he ever going to get her to believe in herself? "You still think this is about some game?" He was furious and wanted to reach out and shake her, but he kept his hands right where they were.

"I don't know, honestly, but I've known Henry a long time. He's a good man and wouldn't treat me in the way you said."

"And you think I would?" He heard the door squeak, and Susan Parker appeared, standing with Scarlett and Mason, watching, listening, and very much getting an earful.

"Well, no, I didn't say that," she said quietly. "I just don't know what to think about the situation, so I've decided not to decide anything. I'll make you breakfast, we'll have coffee, and I'm going to Henry's for dinner tonight, and after that…" She shrugged, and he could see she was struggling to figure out her next step. "I don't know."

The doubts that had been planted by Henry still lingered. What could he do? What could he say to change that? He lifted his hands in surrender. "Promise me one thing."

She shrugged. "It depends."

Of course it did. He couldn't help the chuckle that left him. She was a woman who wouldn't bend easily and wasn't about to give in to anything. "I want to date you, I want to get to know you, but I won't play second to any guy just like you wouldn't play second to another woman. You're going to have to decide, him or me," he said. Then he took in her family standing at the foot of the stairs and could see that the Parkers had heard everything they'd said.

Chapter Fifteen

Ivy was wiping her hands on the dishtowel, watching a shirtless Chris from the kitchen window. He was in the tiny shed out back that housed the water tank and pump from the well, which had broken during breakfast when Naomi had turned on the tap to make coffee. Here was Chris, in back with her father's tools, taking apart the pump and fixing whatever it was that had given out. Scarlett was behind him, pretending to help by handing tools, but at the same time Ivy didn't miss the way her sister ogled every part of him. As good as he looked in a shirt, he looked better without one, and Scarlett…Ivy was ready to strangle her.

She heard the screen door slap.

"Chris said to turn the water on and see if anything comes out," Naomi said.

At least she could do that much. She flicked the tap, and then there was a spurt of water followed by dirt and air. Then the water started flowing.

"Hallelujah, thank you, Chris!" Naomi shouted and

slid open the kitchen window. "Hey, Chris, you frickin' amazing guy, you did it. Water's running."

He lifted the wrench, and Ivy watched as he moved back into the shed. So did Scarlett.

"That little shit," Ivy said. "What does she think she's doing, chasing after Chris like that? Does she have no shame?" She was jealous, and at the same time she felt betrayed by her sister draping herself all over Chris. How could she?

"She's our sister," Naomi said. "You need to set her in her place, Ivy. That man is seriously hot, and she somehow thinks she has a shot." She leaned against the counter. "Tell me, are you with Chris or not? Still can't believe you're actually dating two guys, or are you?"

Ivy turned away from the window, taking in Naomi, who was looking a little rough today. Her hair was in a long ponytail, and she had dark shadows under her eyes. She was again in a loose sweater and jeans, and Ivy was sure she hadn't showered today. "You feeling okay?" she asked and reached out to place her hand on a warm forehead.

Naomi batted it away. "Seriously, stop that. I'm fine. Just a few too many late nights, and I'm talking about you, so don't change the subject."

She didn't know what to say. "I'm not dating them, per say, just dinner with Henry at his place, and then there's Chris. I don't know what the hell this is with him. He lives in Kansas, called me up, drove all the way back here to take me to dinner." She was still trying to make sense of all this. "Dating is something long term. This is just dinner, two guys who are both set on screwing the other over."

Now she had her sister's attention. Naomi glanced out the window to Chris and then slowly back to her. "What do you mean, screwing each other over?"

Ivy rested her hand on the edge of the counter and pushed away, moving over to the table, which was cluttered with unwashed dishes. She pulled out a chair and sat down, watching Naomi, who leaned back against the counter. "Henry asked me for dinner to his place tonight, and on Wednesday he walked me out and asked what I was doing on Thursday, because he wanted to do something with me. I told him I already had plans with someone else. Of course he didn't let it drop, though I still can't understand why.

"He pressed until I told him Chris was coming back and taking me out for dinner, and then he kind of went off on me, saying how Chris was toying with me and wasn't the kind of guy who dated someone like me. Said guys like Chris get off on messing around with girls like me." She stared at her fingers on the table because she had a hard time saying the whole story out loud in her parents' kitchen. Judging by the shocked expression on Naomi's face, she clearly understood the implication.

Naomi turned to the kitchen window, seeing Chris still out back. Then she shook her head as if she couldn't piece together the picture. "Your doctor friend said what, specifically, about Chris? What exactly are we talking about here, Ivy, that Chris is some sadist?" Naomi jabbed her finger in the air to the window. Her gaze was so intent, and now Ivy had to wonder what can of worms she'd just opened, because Naomi would now question and dig and demand answers.

"I'm just saying that Henry implied it was a game, this…whatever this is, for guys like Chris. How he would know this, I have no idea, but then I told Chris—"

"Wait!" Naomi interrupted, gesturing with the flat of her hand. "You talked to Chris about what this doctor friend of yours said?" she hissed.

There was an eighteen-month difference in age between Ivy and Naomi, and Ivy could read her sister well. Right now, Naomi's face let her know she was horrified at what Ivy was saying, and it was at that moment that she realized she shouldn't have said anything at all. She wished she could dial back time to moments ago and keep her mouth shut. Too late. "I did, last night when he came. I just blurted it out and asked him what he wanted from me, and he kind of freaked after I shared everything Henry said about him. Of course he completely lost it, and I didn't expect for him to turn the tables, saying Henry was the problem…"

Naomi's eyes were wide, her mouth gaped in shock, and her hand was in the air. "What the hell!" she said and then slapped her hand over her mouth.

"And then he kissed me," Ivy said. She might as well tell it all.

Naomi let her hand fall to her side. "Chris?" she said.

Ivy could only nod. "Yeah, Chris kissed me, and now I have a dinner date with Henry, but Chris is intent on staying another night and has issued an ultimatum, forcing me to make a choice."

Naomi moved away from the sink and took the chair opposite, reaching over and pressing her hand over hers. "You have two men, by the sounds of it, in a pissing contest over you," she said. Then she patted her hand again. "Nice."

"So who do I choose, the stable reliable guy I know who will give me a respectable and secure future or the guy who sets my heart on fire?" she said. When Naomi looked over to her, she just shook her head. Then there was the fact that both men, according to the other, had motives that could be questionable.

"One woman, two men," Naomi said. "I guess what you need to find out is who the real deal is. Who can you see yourself with twenty, thirty years down the road? Then I believe you'll have your answer."

Chapter Sixteen

H e'd fixed the well, warded off Scarlett's numerous advances as she continued to dog his heels, and was now in Naomi's cabin, under her sink, fixing what she'd said was a blocked pipe. And where was Ivy? Off in her cabin, getting ready for her dinner date with Henry. He twisted the pipe with the plumber's wrench, and water spilled out all over his face.

"Oh, I'm so sorry! Let me get you a towel," Naomi said. She was standing just inside the door and pulled a towel off the rack as he slid out from under the sink.

Water poured out of the loosened pipe he'd just undone. He wiped his face and pulled off the elbow, seeing wadded toilet paper jammed deep inside. He put the bucket under the pipe to catch the remaining water, then stood up and worked at getting the paper out. "So how do you figure all this tissue got jammed way down in here?" he said as he dumped it in the trash and then secured the elbow back in place.

"Really, tissue? Well, I wonder."

Yeah, he wondered, all right. He glanced over to

Naomi, whose expression was suspicious. The plumbing emergency had seemed so urgent and had happened all of a sudden. He dumped the plumber's wrench back in Robert Parker's toolkit and slid out from under the sink again, his faded T-shirt damp. He'd have to change, but at the same time he was glad to keep busy. "So you're set," he said, wiping his hands and then squatting down to mop the floor with the damp towel. He lay back down to check the pipe one last time.

"So Ivy has a date with Henry Blackwell, head of obstetrics, at his house tonight," she said.

He banged his head on the lip of the sink. "Shit!" he yelled as he rubbed his head. Then he stood, glaring down at Naomi.

She winced. "Oh, are you okay?" At least she didn't try to touch him, unlike Scarlet, who'd have been all over him right about now.

"Fine," he said, reaching down to pick up the toolkit to leave, but Naomi was still standing in the doorway.

"I've never met Henry, but I Googled him," she said. "Not really much to look at. I do know Ivy has known him a long time. He's worked with her from her first day as a nurse in obstetrics. Why do you think he said what he did about you?"

He'd thought Naomi was so quiet, kept to herself, but now she was probing, questioning. "Good question. You may want to ask him about it. Excuse me," he said, and she moved aside. He stepped out of the bathroom, the box of tools in hand.

"I would actually like to ask him, but I guess I'd like to ask you why you said the same about him."

He rested the tools at the door and turned to Naomi, realizing Ivy may have shared everything with her sister. Maybe that was what sisters did, share every intimate detail of their lives. It made him feel as if others were intruding into something personal. "She told you everything?"

By the way her face colored, he had his answer. She moved her head as if to get some control and took an awkward step, then opened her mouth as if to elaborate.

He held up his hand. "Stop. You don't need to repeat it." He rested his hands on his hips and glanced to the kitchen, the stairs. The cabins were designed identically but furnished differently. Naomi liked blues and greens, overstuffed cushions.

"You know something, don't you," she said. "This isn't just two guys messing with my sister." Her arms were crossed, and she stepped closer, determined.

"Yeah, I know something."

She took another step closer, her gaze intense. "Is this something you know for a fact, or are you just guessing?"

He shook his head and had to suppress a sarcastic laugh. "Something I overheard from the good doc." He didn't miss the concern and worry that now filled Naomi's expression. "Henry Blackwell isn't who Ivy thinks he is. I was there at the bar the first night she was out with him. Long story, but I'll skip right to it. He was running his mouth to the bartender about his plans for Ivy, you know, to change her into his image of her—but only after he test drives her." He didn't mention the talk about sex, about whatever depraved thing he could get her to do. Maybe some girls liked that, and maybe he was making too big a deal of it, but something about it had bothered him and still did. "You get the picture?"

Her mouth was still wide. "So all the talk about power and control and breaking her down…" She trailed off. He knew she had some idea, but at the same time he wondered how much these sisters really understood about that kind of manipulation, living as sheltered as they were.

"With submission, there are degrees," he said. "There's just talk, one guy to another, but this was different. Do you think a guy who mouths off to someone else about his plans for a woman is who you want for your sister?"

"Of course not, but what about you? According to Ivy, he believes you have an agenda with her. I mean, seriously…" She gestured to him. "Look at you. You're attractive and fit. What is it you want with my sister? Can you honestly tell me you want her for who she is?"

He saw her face the moment she stopped herself from adding anything more, as if Ivy could be somehow less of person because of her weight, as if her plumpness changed how he could feel about her. He was shaking his head. "Do you really think so little of Ivy? You're her sister. You talk about her and insinuate that she's somehow obese and grotesque when nothing could be further from the truth. You should have her back. You know who I see? I see a lady who isn't scoping out how she can get me into bed, someone who isn't looking in the mirror at least twenty, thirty times because she's in love with her image, someone who isn't cruel to others or vindictive. I see someone thoughtful, real, and for the first time I see a lady who interests me, a woman I want to be with. And you know what, Naomi? It really offends me to have Scarlett throwing herself at me right in front of Ivy and then to hear her sisters cutting her up or commenting on the size of her ass or thighs as if that makes her any less of a person. To me, she's perfect. Shame on you."

He swept his hand in the air, taking in the shock in Naomi's expression and her red cheeks. She should have been embarrassed. He pulled open the door and lifted the tools. "And next time you want to talk to me, just be honest. Don't go jamming a bunch of tissue down your drain to have me needlessly fixing something that doesn't need to be fixed."

When he stepped out, he saw Ivy striding to her car, dressed in a blue floral sundress, a light sweater overtop. She looked like a million bucks as she climbed into her small car, started it, and then drove away, and when he glanced down to Naomi, who was now beside him, watching the trail of dust, he could see her humility.

"You're right, and I'm sorry. I deserved that," she said. Her arms were crossed, and she was looking up at him. "Chris, don't let her slip away. She may be scared, and you need to tell her everything Henry said, everything you heard—and if she won't listen, you need to make her."

Chapter Seventeen

Henry's home was two levels, with a sloped circular drive bordered by hedges and trees and loads of privacy, judging by the size of the property. His black Mercedes was parked in front of a closed garage attached to the house, which was anything but ordinary. She pressed the doorbell, and the door opened to reveal a warmly smiling and well-dressed Henry, sporting black tailored pants and a short-sleeved dressy shirt that added something to him she'd never seen before.

"You found it okay?" He stepped back as she strode in, feeling a little overdressed. "Oh man, wow, you look fantastic." He actually gestured to her before resting his hand on her lower back, leaning in, and kissing her. It wasn't lingering, but it promised more to come.

"Yeah, it was… Your directions were easy to follow. Wow, this is an impressive neighborhood. You said you bought this from a doctor?" She was a little rattled and uneasy. It was the kiss, that was all. She knew he wanted to date her—maybe.

"Retired doctor who moved down to Florida. Come on in. Can I get you a drink? Wine, beer, something harder?"

She followed him down a wide hall that opened into a gourmet kitchen with granite counters and dark cabinets, and she looked up to see a vaulted ceiling. A loft or something overlooked the kitchen, which opened to a living room with furnishings that appeared both comfortable and pricey. "You know what? I'm driving, so water would be good," she said.

He gave her a look, and she could see the wine in the rack behind her. Another on the counter was already opened with two glasses. He lifted the bottle and poured out the red. "Nonsense. You have to try this. It's from a northern Italian grape that, as far as I'm concerned, makes this the best red ever." He was holding the glass out to her as if she hadn't said no. She stepped forward and took it as he pulled out one of four plush padded counter stools. "Sit while I work on dinner," he said. She did, and then he lifted his wine and tapped her glass with his. "To the first of many dinners." He took a sip, his blue eyes filled with humor and something else that was intent and focused on her. She lifted the glass and sipped. He was right; it was very good.

"So, dinner. What are you making, again?" she asked. The wood block cutting board had onions, fresh garlic, and artichokes.

He lifted a container from the huge double fridge, and she could see a pan steaming on the gas stove behind him. "Paella. Hope you like spicy and are not opposed to meat." He rested on the counter some cleaned tiger prawns, a large sausage, mussels, and lobster tails. The scent from the stove had her mouth watering.

"I do, but not too scorching."

He smiled as he rinsed the shrimp and mussels. "Fair

enough. You'll love this, though. The chorizo has a bit of a kick. The butcher I use spices it for me perfectly." Then he was chopping and stirring, adding the ingredients to the pot. He really did know his way around a kitchen, and comfortably, too. How old was he, exactly? Forty-three, she was sure she'd heard someone say. She took another sip of wine.

"I just can't get over how lovely you are," he said. "Your hair, that dress." He had great hands, and she noticed his dark hair appeared freshly cut, with less gray, too, she thought.

"Thank you." She ran her hand over the cotton straps, flicking back her hair. She was sitting straight, holding her stomach in, wishing it were flatter than it was. When she glanced up, she realized he was watching her intently.

"So what about cooking? Do you do much?" he asked.

"Not that much. My mother is a great cook. Me, not so much, not something that interested me." However, as she took in his kitchen, she could see it being more fun in a place like this. "I'm more concerned with getting something on the table, nothing fancy. But, from what I'm smelling here, I think I'm in for a treat tonight," she said.

He didn't smile, but his expression held something that had her swallowing and taking another drink. He lifted the bottle and poured more in her empty glass.

"Oh, no, I shouldn't have more. I have to drive," she said, but he was still pouring and then filled his own.

"You'll be fine. Some food, and by then you'll be okay. Trust me. I won't let anything happen."

She relaxed a bit. "Easy for you to say, but this is dangerous stuff, too good, and I'm enjoying it way too much."

He stepped around the counter after flicking off the stove and held out his hand. She wasn't familiar with this

Henry, who seemed to ooze with a strength she'd never imagined was there.

"Oh, okay, are we…?" She put her hand in his, startled, losing her train of thought.

He took her glass and set it on the counter. "Come," he said, leading her out wide French doors to an impressive pool with glistening water, a diving board at one end, and steps in the center. There was an outdoor kitchen barbecue area, chairs, and loungers. It was a dream backyard, and he was still holding her hand. He pulled out a chair at the table set, and she sat down.

"I thought we'd have dinner here. Sit. I'll dish up and bring it out." His hand rested on her shoulder, and he started back into the house.

"Are you sure you don't want me to carry anything?"

"Just stay there, relax," he called out from inside before appearing again with their two glasses in one hand and the bottle in the other. "Here's yours," he said, putting the glasses down in the center and the bottle in a wine bucket at the side. Then he was gone in the house again. A moment later, he returned with two steaming bowls peppered with large chunks of seafood. It smelled heavenly, and it tasted even better.

"I can't remember the last time I had lobster, even these prawns," she said. The mussels she wasn't such a fan of, but she took a bite anyway. She could have cleaned her plate but forced herself to stop eating halfway through. "That was fantastic."

He was already done, leaning back, drinking his wine. She couldn't remember ever having felt so relaxed. It had to be the wine. He really was perfect, perfect for her. He folded up his napkin and rested it on the table, then finished his wine, set his glass down, and slid back his chair. He held out his hand to her again. "Come," he said.

"Okay." She set her hand in his and stood up, a little lightheaded.

His arm was around her back, his hand on her waist, touching her as he walked her over the pool deck. "Do you swim?" he asked, and she couldn't take her eyes off the pool. She was dying to get into it, but thinking of how she looked in a swimsuit had her rethinking the idea.

"I do. Can't say I have in years, though."

"Well, I hope you'll enjoy my pool."

"Yeah, well, me and bathing suits aren't exactly friendly right now," she said and laughed.

He stopped, stepping in front of her, and his expression was unreadable and had her throat thickening. Good Lord, there was something here with Henry she hadn't expected. "It's something that can be changed, you know," he said. "I can help."

She had to think for a minute what he meant by that before it hit her. She blushed and was about to step back.

"You need to be happy with who you are. It bothers you, so change it," he said before stepping in, his hand on her face. Lowering his head, he kissed her.

Chapter Eighteen

The sun was up as Ivy drove past her parents' house and parked in front of her cottage. She didn't miss the fact that her father and Chris were standing behind his pickup, watching her drive in, and Mason was lifting a laundry basket from around the side of the house. She stepped out of her Honda in yesterday's sundress, needing a shower, a change of clothes, and a couple of hours to hide out.

She heard a squeak of a door, knowing it was her parents' house, but didn't look to see who it was as she hurried to her cabin. She expected someone to say something, call to her, anything. Almost there. The door handle was in her hand.

There was a footstep behind her, a creak on the step that had her turning as she stepped in the doorway. Chris, it had to be, and he had every right to be mad. But it wasn't Chris. Worse, it was her father, and the way he was looking at her had her feeling as if she were a teenager who'd broken curfew.

"Hey, Daddy, you probably want to know why I'm

coming in now?" Her voice squeaked. She shouldn't have to explain to anyone. She was a grown woman, entitled to do whatever she wanted.

"Have a lot of questions, I guess." He followed her in, and she put her purse and keys on the table, then instantly wanted to pick them up just to have something in her hands. "You have a good time last night?" he said. Of all the things to ask.

"I did, actually. Henry made a nice dinner, and I had wine. Didn't want to drive, so that's why…" She let her voice trail off. Her dad said nothing. Why was she explaining?

"You stay the night at the good doctor's house?" he said.

After Henry had told her she couldn't drive, he'd taken her keys away. He'd apologized but had said he had to put his foot down.

"I did. In his guest room," she said. At his insistence. She hadn't expected that, considering she'd have slept with him, she thought, if he'd pushed it. She'd never known he could kiss like that. He'd tasted her, kissing her neck and caressing her without fully unclothing her. It had been so hot, and the way he touched her had made her realize his control. He'd stopped, leaving her wanting, before tucking her into the guestroom bed and kissing her tenderly just once more before pulling the door closed. Her face heated now thinking of it. Her father was watching her, and then there was another squeak. This time it was Chris, and she felt horrible.

"I've got some things to do. Chris here wants to have a word with you, and then, if you have a moment, Ivy." That was all her father said as he pushed open the door and stepped outside. It was something he'd said to her only a time or two as a teen.

Then there were two.

Tension thickened the air, and all that flirty chemistry that had been there just the day before was gone. Whatever Chris was thinking or feeling, she hadn't a clue except that he wasn't the friendly, happy Chris who wanted her.

"We were worried," he said. "I suppose you didn't see the messages? No one here knows where he lives, so you can imagine how worried your parents were."

She opened her purse and rummaged, but she didn't see her cell phone. "I must have left it at Henry's," she said. She hadn't take it out of her purse, though, so where was it? She touched her head. "I'm sorry. Maybe I lost it." She was thinking. She'd used it for directions. She'd put it in her purse.

The expression on his face was hard.

"I'm sorry. I really did drink too much wine. I shouldn't have."

He was nodding, and he glanced to the door. "I'm sure without a doubt you did." The way he said it, she knew he was implying something else.

"It wasn't Henry," she said.

He raised an eyebrow. His entire face said he didn't believe her. "Really, who poured? You, him?"

Even after that kiss, her glass had been filled. He'd handed it to her, not asked her. She'd said nothing.

"Yeah, just as I thought," Chris said. Then he started to the door, and a profound sadness hit her.

"I'm sorry. I didn't sleep with him," she said. She would have, though, and she knew it, but this morning when she'd woken in that very comfortable, spacious guestroom without a stitch of clothing on, alone, she'd been grateful she hadn't.

Then he was in her face again, but he wasn't angry. She wished he would yell at her, something, because then she'd know he still cared, still wanted her. Except what she saw hurt more: resignation.

"But you would have, and he could have easily had you, right?" he said. "I can tell by your face. I guess I have my answer." That was all he said before he stepped outside the screen door, letting it slap closed behind him.

"Chris!" She followed, and he stopped in the dirt, looking back at her. What could she say to him that would make this better? She was hit with this awful feeling that she had cheated on him, but that was ridiculous. "That's not fair. It was just dinner," she said.

This time he did smile as he shook his head, but it was sad, and she knew he wasn't going to listen. "Keep telling yourself that, but you're a big girl, and you walked into something with both eyes wide open. Maybe this is what you want, him, that, but I won't play second." He glanced to the side, his hands on his hips. "I'm heading out. I'm going home. I really hope you know what you're doing."

Then he was walking away.

Chapter Nineteen

He stalked back to Taz's cottage and took the steps up two at a time. He packed his clothes in his bag and was halfway down the stairs when Scarlett walked in, wearing indecently short cutoffs and a tank top that plunged, showing her cleavage. Yeah, she had a great body, curvy, toned, and she flashed him a killer smile that screamed trouble.

"Scarlett," he said. He noted she was barefoot as she closed the inside door behind her and leaned against it. Of course now every one of his alarm bells was going off. "What are you doing?"

She shrugged and rested her hand on her hip. She was trying to play a woman's role, teasing him, and she was headed for a load of trouble.

"Your parents know you're in here?" he said and started into the bathroom.

"What my momma and daddy don't know won't hurt them," she said.

He packed up his shaving kit and walked back out to

where she was now at the table, her hands in his bag, touching his clothes.

"Why are you leaving?" she said. Her big eyes, round face, and pouty lips would have made any other guy have her flat on that table, clothes stripped, taking her up on her sexual offer, taking everything she somehow thought she wanted to give away. He wondered, though. It wouldn't come free, not from Scarlett. Even as young and immature as she was, he suspected she could turn a man's life and sanity upside down, but that wouldn't be before the wrong man taught her a lesson she wasn't ready to learn.

"It's time for me to go," he said. "I have a life in another state and a business I need to get back to."

She didn't move when he reached his bag and put his shaving kit inside. She stayed where she was, leaning against the table, looking up at him. Then her hand was on his arm, running up, and he could feel her studying him. He gazed down, and he realized that if she weren't a Parker and this were somewhere else, he'd have taken what she offered and then kept right on walking—but this was one of the sisters. He reached over, took her hand, and set it down.

"She doesn't want you, but I do," she said. "I could give you what you want."

He stepped back, zipped up his bag, and looped it over his shoulder. Then he walked over to the door and pulled it open. "Scarlett, you think so little of your sister. What is it Ivy has done to you that you hate her so much you would throw yourself at me even though you know I'm here for her?"

She appeared rattled, and the sexual energy she'd been giving off moments before dialed back a bit. She crossed her arms over her stomach. She was thinking again.

Another angle? "I don't hate my sister. Why would you say that?"

"You act like it. How do you think Ivy feels, all the remarks you've made, all of you making her feel less than? I've lost count of the number of implications you've made about her size, her weight. She has feelings, and not once have I heard her say one cruel, hurtful thing to any of you, so what gives? What is this about, you throwing yourself at me? You're how old, seventeen, eighteen?" Walking trouble and not his problem. And damn Ivy for worrying him the way she had. He'd forced her to choose, and she'd done just that. Maybe he didn't know her and this really was what she wanted. Whatever, he was done. He had a life in Kansas and enough pride still to know when it was time to go.

Scarlett's cheeks were pink, and she wasn't trying to show anything off to him now. "I'm old enough, almost done school. I just thought..." Then she stopped talking, but he could see she was thinking of something else.

"You thought, what, offer up sex and you can steal me away from your sister?"

"No, of course not!"

"Really?" He took a step closer as she held her arms tighter, slouching a bit to hide everything she'd exposed. "I like Ivy. You're just the kid sister," he said. He knew it was cruel and could see how she'd taken it much like a slap to the face. "And a word of advice, Scarlett: If you flaunt yourself with as much skin as you're showing, like a two-bit whore, that's how guys will treat you."

Her eyes flashed with hurt, anger, and shock.

He pushed open the screen door and stepped out, and he didn't look back.

Chapter Twenty

His truck was gone by the time she'd showered and pulled on a pair of jeans and a loose cotton shirt. She'd stalled long enough, and she walked over to her parents' house, feeling emptiness and loss as she strode up the steps.

"Hey!"

She jumped, hearing Scarlett's voice and seeing her in the wicker chair in the corner. "You scared me," she said, her hand on the screen door.

"Daddy's in the house with Mama. They're waiting for you. You worried everyone, you know."

Ivy's hand was shaking, and she gripped it. She hadn't thought to phone home. She should have, but she was how old? "I was fine. Just had too much wine, so I didn't drive."

Scarlett wasn't smiling, and it wasn't lost on Ivy that she was wearing more clothes today than she normally did, blue jeans and a T-shirt that actually covered her. It seemed as if everything here had changed overnight. "They called the hospital this morning. I heard them calling your cell phone I don't know how many times."

"Why?" She moved away from the door, and her heart kicked up another notch.

"You didn't answer, and Mama wanted to call the sheriff, but Daddy said no. No one knew where the doctor you're dating lives. Then Chris called someone and got the doctor's address, and then you drove in just when Daddy and Chris were going to show up at his house."

Her hands were on her cheeks as she tried to take in the horror of the situation. Then she heard the screen door, footsteps, and there was her father.

He glanced once to Scarlett. "You have things to do that don't include you sitting out here, sticking your nose in your sister's business," he said, and Scarlett was up, off the steps, and around the house. Her father stepped outside, holding the door wide. "Ivy," he said and gestured for her to go in.

She stepped in, a voice in her head saying she was twenty-six, she was old enough, she shouldn't be answering to anyone. She was an adult, and she needed to set some ground rules. But she said none of that as she noted her mom in the kitchen at the table. Her dad sat in his chair, and Ivy took the one to his right, looking across from her mom.

"You worried us to death, Ivy. You should have called. Why didn't you call?" her mom asked and then stood up, her hand on her dad's shoulder.

"Give us a minute," her dad said to her mom, who went down the hall and seemed to busy herself in the laundry room.

"I'm sorry," Ivy said. "It wasn't intentional. I should have phoned, but I didn't think of it, as it wasn't a big deal. I just had too much wine, and I stayed in the guest room. I must have left my phone there." And somehow turned off the ringer? She still wasn't sure how that had happened.

"You're home now, but we didn't know where you were. We didn't have his number, didn't know where he lived. Chris found out, made some calls, and we called the doctor's house but got his voicemail, so you could only imagine our concern. We were about to drive in to find you when you pulled in."

Of course she felt horrible. "Chris did that?"

"He's a good man, complex, an overcomer, you know. He may not have all the flash that this doctor has, who I don't know—but at the same time, Ivy, I know enough."

"Dad, I don't know what Chris told you about Henry…"

Her dad touched her hand on the table and leaned in, shaking his head. "Chris never said a word. It was Naomi. Maybe Chris had a right to be worried, maybe he didn't, but what I'm saying is that I don't know this Henry Blackwell. I know nothing about him. But Chris is a man I know a lot more about. He grew up with nothing. He joined the military because that was the only option he had. He's seen things he wishes he hadn't. He didn't have things handed to him, and he doesn't act as if the world owes him anything."

"So what are you saying? Because Chris is gone, if you didn't notice. There isn't a chance with him now, anyway." She realized now that this made everything about the situation even worse. It was the thought that she may have messed up any chance of having something with Chris.

"No, but we don't know about Doctor Blackwell, either. You want to date him, you bring him home for dinner here. You bring him to meet your mother and me." Then he scooted back his chair and looked down at her one last time. "You're a grown woman, Ivy, but you don't know everything about men, what they want or what they're thinking. I may have sheltered you a little too much, but I didn't want you or your sisters to experience much of the bad out there, and maybe that was my mistake."

Chapter Twenty-One

"Twice in one day," Henry said as he held open his door. He was barefoot in a pair of jeans and a white golf shirt. He stepped back. He looked good.

"Sorry I didn't call. I, ah, think I may have left my phone here," Ivy said.

The blue in his eyes was filled with teasing, and then he winked. "You did. Found it while cleaning up." He strode to the back of the house. Music was playing. He stopped in the kitchen. "Was just going to make myself a latte, how about you?" He tossed her an easy smile again, resting his hands on the counter. He didn't look away, and instead of filling in the awkward silence, he allowed his gaze to linger over all of her.

She swallowed. "Sure."

"Great." He winked again as he took a beautiful teal mug from his cupboard and poured coffee beans in an impressive espresso machine. Of course he had money, and it oozed everywhere, the comfort.

"I hope you had fun last night," he added as he worked

his machine. The coffee smelled great, and he poured milk into a metal carafe to steam.

"I did," she said, but she felt guilty at the same time. "Hey, I wanted to ask you something. My family was trying to get a hold of me. They said they called here, and that was after they kept calling my cell."

He pulled open a kitchen drawer, lifted out her cell phone, and slid it over to her. "Before I forget," he said and went back to making the lattes. She touched the screen and saw the voicemails, then noted the ringer was turned off. "I haven't checked my voicemail, day off. All emergencies call my cell phone," he said over his shoulder as if it were no big deal. "Here you go, enjoy." He winked at her again. "Join me out by the pool. It's such a beautiful day."

"You know what? I really should be going. I just came to get this, and I have things to do at home before my shift tomorrow."

"Nah, that can wait. It's a long drive. Come on out. Drink your coffee at least." He gestured outside. He really was friendly and made everything easy.

She followed him out and took a seat in a padded chair. He sat across from her.

"You said your family was calling," he said. "Is everything okay?"

What could she say? They were freaking out because she hadn't come home. "It is. It's just they didn't know where I was. I should have phoned. That was my fault."

He rested his coffee on the table. "I'm so sorry, Ivy. That's my fault. I insisted you stay, and I should have known to take care and call your family." He lifted his hands. "I'll be sure next time they know."

Next time, was he kidding? She squeezed her legs together, because last night she'd have slept with him, and she could feel how he wanted to just handle it all. She could sense for a moment how easy it would be to just let him. "You know my parents don't know you, and…"

He put his coffee down again and gestured to her. "Say no more. I should meet them, and I will." He reached over, rested his hand on her arm, and caressed her. Then he stood up and was in front of her, holding out his hand. "Come here," he said. It was in his expression, how sure he was of himself, as she lifted her hand. He took it in his and pulled her up.

She was standing toe to toe with him as he held her cheeks, leaned in, and kissed her again, so soft. He deepened it as he just held her as if she were something precious. It was nice, but it didn't sizzle and didn't take her breath away. Last night had been different. It must have been the wine.

"Come swimming with me," he said as he allowed his hands to run over her shoulders and down.

"I didn't bring a bathing suit." She laughed.

The smile he had turned wicked. "Who needs a bathing suit?"

This time she stepped back when his meaning came clear. "Yeah, I'm not comfortable with that." She laughed, and so did he.

"Of course you are. Last night you were begging for me." His hand was at the edge of her T-shirt, lifting.

"No." She put her hand over his and stepped away. He stood where he was, but he didn't take his gaze from her, and he didn't appear apologetic.

"Come here." He gestured toward her, but she shook her head as she stepped back again.

"Did you take my phone last night?" she said. It was crazy. Of course he'd say no.

He took another step and then stopped, his hands on his hips. He wasn't Chris. If there were ever two men who were absolute opposites, they were Chris and Henry. One polished, the other rough.

"You took my phone," she said. He hadn't answered, and she really didn't like the way he was looking at her now. It was something she'd never seen in his expression before.

"I didn't want you woken," he said.

Her hand rested over her chest. "It was in my purse. Did you go through my purse? Why would you do that? And the wine…I told you I had to drive, but you kept pouring it, and—"

"I have a lot to offer the right woman. Yes, you had wine, and you chose to drink it. I didn't make you. Do you think I would allow someone I care about to walk out that door and get behind the wheel and drive? I could have had you last night, but I want you sober the first time I have you, the first time you get on your knees. I know you want it too. You think I couldn't tell your reaction to me?" He didn't move closer to her. In fact, he stayed where he was, and then he held out his hand to her. "Come here," he said, his meaning clear, and she realized then how wrong she'd been.

She shook her head, turned away, and walked back into the kitchen, where she grabbed her phone and purse. She didn't glance back as she walked out the door.

Chapter Twenty-Two

His phone was ringing again as he climbed out of the shower. Whoever kept calling was determined, considering it was late, after midnight. He grabbed a towel and strode out of his boxlike bathroom to his small bedroom, where his cell phone was lying on top of yesterday's clothes piled on his unmade bed. Light filtered in from the hall.

"Hello," he snapped, not in the mood to handle another problem. He was tired and pissed and just wanted to crawl into bed and sleep.

"Chris, it's Ivy."

He sighed, holding the phone but pulling the receiver down. He swiped his hand over his forehead. Dealing with any of the Parkers tonight was far down on the list of things he had any desire to do.

"Ivy, it's late," he said, wiping his face and dragging the towel over his head to dry his hair.

"I've been calling and you haven't answered, and I didn't know what to do…"

Why was he hearing noise and traffic in the background? "Where are you?" he asked.

"I'm outside a gas station. I forgot my charger, and my cell phone is dead, so I'm using a pay phone. I'm in Kansas."

"What, why? Did something happen?" What the hell was going on? "Where exactly are you?"

"Just off the freeway at the west side. I'm sorry, Chris. I wanted to talk to you, and I know this probably sounds crazy…" She was rambling, and he had some idea where she was as he took down the address.

"I can come and get you." He reached for his jeans and sat on the bed, his phone between his shoulder and ear.

"I can come to you," she said. "I just don't know where you live."

Of course she didn't. He relayed his address and directions that would have her outside his house in half an hour, give or take, except he realized too late it was pouring rain. As he waited, the clock ticking, he couldn't help worrying. He should have insisted on going to her. Considering the hour and her dead cell phone, if something happened, she wouldn't be able to reach him.

He watched from his front window: forty minutes, forty-five. The rain pelted the ground. Shit, what was wrong with him? He should have gone to her.

Then he saw headlights and pulled open the door. He strode out in his old sneakers, jeans, and a T-shirt, not bothering with a coat or the fact that he was soaked by the time he reached the street. Headlights blinded him, windshield wipers flicked back and forth, and he waved as the car pulled to the curb and parked behind his pickup. He walked around to the driver's side as she turned off the engine, and he pulled open her door, taking in something in her expression that seemed so unsure and hesitant. He wanted to pull her out and put his arms around her to hold her, but he had to stop himself. He didn't know why she was here.

She stepped out in loose faded jeans and a T-shirt, her hair tied up in a messy bun. The rain hit her and she didn't seem to notice, and he just stared at her, waiting her out.

"I'm trying to figure out why you're here. Did something happen? What is this?" He was soaked, and she blinked as she glanced up, rain hitting her face like a shower, soaking her. Her T-shirt was sticking to her.

"I had to come and see you, because you were right. I screwed up. I didn't believe you could want me," she said in a voice that was loud enough to hear over rain that drowned out everything else.

"Come on," he said as he took her hand, shoved her door closed, and led her into the house.

"I'm soaked," she said, dropping her purse on the floor by the door.

"I'll grab a towel. Come in." He grabbed one from the bathroom around the corner and stepped back to see her taking in his tiny house. What was she thinking at all the plainness, bargain basement everything? He didn't have a clue. It was a problem for most women.

Then she took the towel he handed her. "Thank you." She rubbed the side of her face softly and then appeared shy, nervous, as she stood before him. He noticed her bare feet, her shoes kicked off at the door. She was so close to him. "I feel horrible for how I treated you." She pressed the towel to her chest and the shirt that was glued to her generous breasts.

"So you drove all this way to tell me you feel bad? That's something you could have done over the phone."

She flinched. He could be an asshole at times without even trying. "You're right, I could have, and maybe that would have been the sane thing to do, but the fact is I didn't, and now I'm here. I didn't know you tried to find me. I'm sorry about last night and everything. Henry took my phone and hid it. I had no idea, and when you were so angry this morning, you had every right to be." She appeared embarrassed, hurt, and she glanced to the side.

"Did he hurt you?" Chris asked. He wanted to kill the guy, because he had worried and now suspected there was more.

"No, just opened my eyes. I never felt as if I were good enough, and I had this doubt that you could really be interested in me. This may sound ridiculous, but I even felt grateful that Henry could be. I still don't know why he said what he did about you, but you haven't lied to me." She was shaking her head.

Chris knew he wasn't making any of this easy.

"That was the first time I've felt as if someone was trying to take away my ability to make a decision, and it terrified me how he was so subtle about it. I found it would be easy to just slip into that and let him decide everything. It cheapened things, and I thought I knew him. How could I have not?"

"He's slick is all, knows what he's doing, but at least you found out and walked away. You did, right?"

Her expression turned furious in an instant. "You must have very little respect for me if you would actually believe I'd come here to see you and then go back and see him. I had dinner with him, and yes, maybe I shouldn't have gone, but we were friends—no, colleagues for so long. I thought I knew him. Then you showed up and rocked my world. No, stop it." She tapped her head. "I'm glad I went, because my eyes are open now. You want me still, or was that just a game? I need to know if it was real."

Did she have no idea how wonderful she was? She was

the first woman he'd ever met who had him feeling everything, wanting her, seeing something in her that told him having her in his life would make it perfect.

"You think I would have tracked you down to play a dating game?" she said.

"Honestly, I don't know what to think. Are you saying you're here because…"

She stepped forward and pressed her hand to the flat of his chest. "I'm here because I choose you, even though it's not a fair choice. I choose you if you still want me, all of me." Her implied insinuation made him angry. She actually stepped back, and he could see how she still couldn't believe she was attractive.

He took a step in, resting his hands over her shoulders and holding her as she looked up with startled, questioning eyes. He could see the plea and the moment she'd put herself out there to him. It was a vulnerability he suspected she didn't display often. "Yes, I want you," he said. "You are perfection to me. That sassy attitude, that light that shines so bright from you, and the fact that you're not calculating. There's so much about you, and it bothers me that you can't see what I see." He turned her and guided her to the mirror at the door. Standing behind her, seeing her, the image of her, her head just topped his shoulders. Something about this felt more right than anything. "I need you to see what I see. You are enough. I need you to say it, believe it, and get it out of your head that your size has somehow made you less. To me, you're perfect, with enough substance that I believe you wouldn't break apart with me. You're the first woman I really believe can go the distance with me."

He took in her startled expression and the lump in her throat as she swallowed, and he took her hand and pulled her into the tiny front room of his small older house. "As you can see, this is it," he said. "I have an old worn sofa—may not look like much, but it's comfortable. And the easy chair, the few things I have here, that's all I need. I don't have much, I don't make much, but I own this house. There's no fanciness and style and comfort. I can't give you that."

She looked at everything and back to him.

"This is just stuff, Chris. It doesn't mean anything. But you…" She faced him and slid her hand over his chest, looking up at him. "You're the one who means everything."

Chris slid his hand around the small of her back and pulled her in closer. "What about work, your job at the hospital?"

She lifted her hands over his shoulder and looped them around his neck. "I called in sick, so I'm yours until we figure things out."

"Hmm" was all he said as he leaned in this time, kissing her deeply before pulling back again and rocking with her in his arms.

Her tongue flicked over lips that were begging for him, where he'd tasted her, and the smile that lit up her face brightened this place, this house, his heart. "So I suppose we need to figure out just one last thing." She gave him a questioning look as she stayed where she was. "Kansas or Wyoming?"

Chapter Twenty-Three

The ringing of the phone stirred Ivy, but she was too tired to do anything about it. She felt Chris's hand on her ass, sliding over her, and she pressed against his warmth, skin to skin. He groaned, and she stayed where she was, eyes shut, as he reached over her.

"Hello?" His voice was rough, tired.

She opened one eye to see it was only seven in the morning. Not much sleep, considering they'd gone to bed at three—no, four. Okay, maybe it had been sometime after five when she'd finally drifted off after a marathon of sex.

"No, what the fuck?" Chris was out of bed and mad, and she turned to see him stride naked out of the bedroom.

Good Lord, he had a great ass and a body that looked even better without clothes. Not only did he have a tattoo on his arm, he had another on his thigh, the army insignia with an eagle. It was impressive, and she'd explored and touched it. For the first time she felt special and cared for by a man. Yes, her thighs weren't as skinny as she'd like, her ass was too big, and her stomach was a little soft, but he'd touched her and connected with her as if none of it mattered—and could the man kiss!

Her hand rested over the thin sheet that covered her, and she wanted to go back to sleep, but at the same time, she'd never felt this good before. She could hear him talking from the living room, and he didn't sound happy. Then he was yelling, and she heard him swear again. No, someone had done something to piss Chris off. She could hear the floor squeak from his footsteps. The house was small, plain, but none of that mattered. This was nothing like Henry's spacious comfortable place with every luxury she could imagine to entice her. This was the first time she realized love was all about the man, and everything else was just stuff.

She didn't know what made her look over to see Chris leaning in the doorway, holding his phone. She couldn't keep herself from staring at his chest and abs, which were a work of art. Strength oozed from him. He wiped his face, and the smile and ease she'd hoped to see wasn't there. He still said nothing, and a voice inside her was screaming that something was seriously off.

"Chris, is everything okay?" She propped herself up on her elbows and then sat up.

"One of my clients' job sites was hit. It's happened four times over the last month, and the damage is pretty bad. Whoever it was did a number on the ventilation unit and sheet metal I supplied." He was rubbing his head and swore again, she could see how pissed he was.

"Your client? So if the client's already paid for the parts…"

He was shaking his head, stalking into the bedroom. He grabbed his jeans from the floor and pulled them on. "Yes, that's the problem. It seems my guys delivered yesterday but didn't get paid, and I'm only hearing about it now because they were promised payment this morning. However, this client seems to have some target on his back and is running into a load of problems. His insurance was cancelled after the last time, so he's out the damage—or rather I'm out, considering my chances of collecting have just dropped to about zero." He grabbed a faded green T-shirt and pulled it on.

"Because you weren't there to make sure…" She trailed off at the dark look he leveled her way.

"I'm a hands-on owner and don't let my guys handle business. This was a first, and my guys know they need to get payment up front, but I guess the client laid on a sob story and promised to pay in the morning."

"And they believed him?" she added, understanding a little and feeling as if some of this was her fault. "I'm sorry."

"For what?" He sounded pissed.

She was about to say it, for him driving out and sticking around to date her, and maybe if he'd been here, this wouldn't have happened. But then what? She'd have been with Henry and never figured out what a scumbag he was. She felt sick for a minute. The bed dipped, and he was beside her. "I don't know," she said, "but you weren't here, you were in Wyoming. I guess I can't really be sorry for that, but I am. Will you be out a lot?" She winced when he shook his head.

"Enough, yeah…" He ran his hand over his head. She could see he was rattled. "I hate to do this, but I need to go take care of this mess and try to salvage something." He leaned in and kissed her, and her hand went to his cheek, feeling the roughness, the whiskers of a man who hadn't shaved. "I don't know how long I'll be, but go back to sleep," he said.

She watched then as he walked out. She heard him grab his keys, and then the door closed. Ivy laid back and reached over to the emptiness beside her, cursing the phone for their interruption. Now she was awake, and no matter how she tried, she was positive she'd never be able to get back to sleep.

Chapter Twenty-Four

I vy had pulled on one of Chris's T-shirts and dumped the previous day's clothes into his dated washer. She hadn't packed a change, considering she'd decided to drive to Kansas on a whim. She had her purse, her wallet, and her dead cellphone, which was charging with Chris's charger. She'd even borrowed his toothbrush after climbing in the shower. Now she heard the door as she stepped out of the small laundry room at the back of the house.

Chris dumped his keys on the small kitchen table and took her in, her bare legs. The edge of his T-shirt barely covered her. He warmed, she thought, but still seemed distracted.

"Hey, you're back. Everything get sorted out?" She couldn't help feeling uneasy and naked, standing there.

He was still staring at her, and she noted the distance. "Not really," he said. She couldn't help wondering if he was bothered that she'd helped herself to his shirt.

"Sorry, I had nothing clean." She gestured back to the laundry room with her thumb. "Helped myself to your shirt and your washer. I hope you don't mind."

He slid past her, his hand on her waist. The simple touch reassured her as he reached for the coffee pot and then opened the cupboard she'd also been about to ransack.

"Of course not, looks great on you," he said and gave her another distracted smile, but she didn't miss the fact that something was off, that something was bothering him. He put on some coffee, and Ivy pulled out a chair and sat down.

"So what happened?" she asked when he didn't offer to share anything else.

He shook his head and opened the fridge to pull out eggs and a slab of bacon. "Out about a hundred twenty grand and change. The order was a big one, one I should have handled myself. My mistake."

The guilt ate away at her. Did he blame her?

"Sorry," she said again, running her hand over her chest and holding it there. She couldn't shake this awkwardness.

"Stop apologizing. None of this is on you. Just never expected this client to pull this, and now he doesn't have the money to pay, and he's gone to another supplier for the replacement parts. Worse, he has no insurance to cover the damaged items because he's had one too many claims this year and six weeks ago his coverage was cancelled, and he said nothing." He was cutting slices of bacon and laying them across a cast iron frying pan. "It's a bad loss."

"And the guys who worked for you, the ones who delivered it?" she asked. Something like this was fireable, maybe.

He shook his head. "They screwed up big time. One said he knew it wasn't a good idea, and the other said they never expected this. The client said he'd forgotten his check but would have it today, so just leave everything. He even said it would be fine with me. They believed him. Should have fired their asses." He was mad. A hundred and twenty grand… She couldn't fathom it. That was a lot of money.

"You didn't, though," she said, and he glanced her way, shaking his head.

"No, but it won't make a difference if I can't pay the bills and end up closing up shop. I still have suppliers I have to pay, loans due, salaries…" He stopped talking as he flipped the bacon, which smelled so good. "How many eggs?"

"Two, thank you."

He set down the fork he'd used to turn the bacon and glanced over to her. "I guess I should be apologizing to you. Taking off, having this mess happen, the timing sucks. I'm sorry. I kind of had plans for today that didn't include putting out fires. You have work, I have this mess here, and we haven't had a chance to talk about what's next for us."

No, they hadn't. She'd called in sick for today, but tomorrow was up in the air.

"You asked last night, Wyoming or here," she said. "I guess we should talk about it. You have a business, I have a career I love, but there are hospitals here, and…"

He was shaking his head. "It may not even be a choice. This loss could sink me."

Then his phone was ringing from where it sat on the kitchen table beside his keys. He reached for it as she helped herself to some coffee, and she listened to the frustration in his voice at whomever he was talking to, knowing his problems now affected her.

Chapter Twenty-Five

"Hey there, you." Chris stroked his cat, Tuffy, who'd appeared through the cat door and was meowing and demanding attention before hopping onto the easy chair and curling up for a day of sleep. Ivy was changing back into her clean clothes, and Chris was trying to figure out what to do next. After choking down a quiet breakfast of bacon and eggs, which had seemed tasteless, he'd drunk three cups of coffee, and the caffeine buzz was now kicking in, which was probably not a good thing, considering his anxiety was already ramped up.

"Cute cat," Ivy said as she stepped into the small boxy living room. "Didn't know you had animals." She wore her light baggy T-shirt and fitted blue jeans, her dark hair brushed straight and loose.

"Cat, one only. The city and my time don't allow for anything else," he said. "So today…"

She held up her hand and stepped in, touching his arm as if to stop him. Her touch was so soft and easy, and at the same time he could feel she was giving everything of herself to him. "You have a lot to worry about. I do, though, need to go home, and I guess we need to decide on where and how this is going to work."

He took a breath. Everything he'd thought would be easy about them, Ivy and Chris, a relationship he'd never expected or wanted, had suddenly taken a huge detour to something more complicated. He wasn't just out a hundred and twenty grand: His credit line was due today, and he'd been counting on that client's payment to keep the cycle of debt in motion and himself afloat. This was his business. Now, unless he could get his bank to give him an extension, he didn't know what he'd do. "Yeah, we do," he said. "I just…" His gut twisted at the thought of deciding something with Ivy now when he had some major fixes to make in his business.

"Last night you said Kansas or Wyoming, but that was before everything went sideways on you this morning."

Her understanding made him wonder where she'd been all his life. He lifted his hand and slid it around her lower back, wanting to lean in and kiss her, but he realized financial problems had completely killed the mood. "Yeah, you're right. As much as I don't like the thought of you driving all the way back to Kansas alone, I get it. But I can't leave today. I have to handle things here, fix this," he said, his arms around her, rocking with her.

"I get it, Chris, I really do. You fix this. But what do you want to do? Do I come back, give notice? We kind of have a distance problem, and you can't manage what's just happened from Wyoming." She swayed against him. "I'll give notice, and I can look for something here," she said, sounding so sure, taking in his small place.

It would make it easier even though he'd been thinking things would go the other way, but then, he hadn't had time to research what it would take to set something up in

Buffalo—the demand, the costs, and whether it was even feasible. Right now, a second location wasn't going to happen, considering his business was doing only marginally better after two years of just getting by. That didn't say much.

He slid his hands over her shoulders, holding her, this woman he could never have imagined himself with. "You surprise me. Any other woman would be freaking out, maybe halfway out the door, but here you are, trying to be reasonable. It really is damn sexy." He took in the hesitation, the blush and the way his words rattled her. "I may not be at the top of my game right now, but having you here has made this morning easier."

She seemed flustered as she wiped her hand over her warmed cheeks. "Oh boy, well, you just know all the right things to say to a girl," she said. "How about this? I'll go back, pack up a few things, and get someone to cover my shifts, and I'll come back in the morning."

It was a great idea, and hopefully it would give him the time he needed to figure out a solution to his dire situation.

He walked her to her car, and she slid behind the wheel, but he leaned in and kissed her, allowing it to linger a moment. Then he closed her door and watched as she drove away. When he went back into the house, the next call he had to make would probably include a lot of begging and pleading—everything he hated to do.

Chapter Twenty-Six

I t was always the same, coming home. The house and everything about her father's property was unchanged. Her parents, her sisters, and the three cottages were exactly as they had been just a day before, but at the same time everything seemed different.

It was her who was different.

Everyone was watching her as she pulled in and parked in front of her cottage. She stepped out to see her father, followed by her mother, walking over. Scarlett and Mason were behind them, and Naomi stepped out of her small cottage, as well. The screen door clattered, and everyone was giving all their attention to her.

"Hi, Daddy, Mama," she said, holding her hand up to the glare of the setting sun.

"Got your message, Ivy, and I have to say I was a little surprised, especially after our talk yesterday morning," her father said.

Her mom was staring at her as if she'd lost her mind. "You drove all the way to Kansas to see Chris, and?" She gestured for Ivy to finish.

"And Chris and I talked." Her face heated, and she cleared her throat, thinking of how Chris had peeled off her wet clothes and looked at her naked for the first time as if she were perfection before he made love to her. "We're going to figure some things out, and we're going to live together," she said, taking in the shock on her parents' faces and hearing a throat clear behind them as Scarlett stepped around her father.

"Live together just like that?" Scarlett said. Ivy ground her jaw, not missing the spite or something that said her sister was jealous as all hell.

"Yes, live together. We just need to work out if it'll be there in Kansas or here."

Naomi jogged up in a plain blue cotton sundress that stopped at her knees. Her hair hung long and loose. "Well, I have to say I'm glad it's Chris and not that doctor. I like Chris."

Mason was nodding as if her two cents were needed. Scarlett, though, crossed her arms, and her expression said loudly that she was far from happy. The little shit was still stuck on Chris. Ivy didn't realize she was fisting her hands tightly until she felt her nails dig into her palms.

"So where is Chris right now?" her father asked.

"He has some work stuff he needs to sort out, and I need clothes. I also need to make arrangements with work for time off if I can, for at least this week. Then I'm going to head back to his place tomorrow. Next week I'll deal with later," she added.

"What's the rush, Ivy?" her mom said. "You've just met the man and are now driving to another state to see him, and then you're, what, going to move in together?" Her mom glanced to her dad, whose face said nothing and everything at the same time.

"Mom, Dad, I know this may sound crazy, but Chris is

the one. I just wouldn't allow myself to believe that a guy like him could love a girl like me." No one was saying anything, and it made her feel as if she were opening herself to scrutiny, to exposure, in a way she never did. She never left herself this open, even with her family. "You know what? This really is my choice," she said, knowing it sounded defensive.

"Just hold on here." Her dad jumped in, and Mason was grinning as if she were really getting into this debate on Ivy's life. "Chris is a fine man. You're right there. But I have to wonder, Ivy, if you really know what you're getting into…"

"Dad," she started, but her dad held up his hand to stop her.

"No, let me finish. This has kind of snowballed. It was one thing for that young man to drive out here to get to know you and to stay here, but you suddenly coming in, packing, and moving to Kansas? This is starting to seem too much like Jerry and Taz. What about your job, the years of college, nursing school? You're going to just give it all up for a man?" Her dad was frowning. She hadn't expected this, and she didn't know how to get him to understand.

"I'm not giving it up for a man, and Taz and Jerry are married. They're in love. I thought you were okay with him, them together?"

"I'm fine with them being married, but they went into it too fast, and you remember what happened. It turned out well, but it very well could have backfired. We said nothing then, but this time, Ivy, I wonder if you can even see what we do. You drive all night, and the next thing you're putting your career second."

Hearing him say it again, she knew deep down she was in fact likely going to give notice and look for a job in

Kansas because she was the girl following the guy. Admitting it to her parents and everyone else, though, was something else entirely. They were right, to a point, but how could she explain that Chris felt like her everything right now, and this was something she had to pursue, a future she wanted? "Okay, maybe to a point you're right, but I'm still a nurse, and there are other hospitals. I never said Kansas was a sure thing, because Chris has said he'd consider moving here."

Her dad smiled, and that surprised her. "Great, good to hear." He leaned in. "Let him move here. He can date you, get to know you. He can stay in Taz's cabin."

Instead of opening her mouth to argue, she was stuck on how Chris would feel about moving to Wyoming. The closest she'd get to sleeping with him would be sneaking in at dark and out before dawn, or him sneaking into her cabin.

Not an easy solution, and not what she'd expected.

Chapter Twenty-Seven

Not only had she not been able to get the day off, but Chris hadn't taken too well to her dad's demand. In fact, he'd said nothing about it after a second or two of silence other than that he'd have to call her back, as he had meetings and problems he still needed to sort out. Now here she was, checking her cell phone for the fourth time this morning as she climbed out of her car in the hospital employee parking lot. Still no call. Maybe he was mad, or maybe a night away and distance had changed his mind. "Stop it," she snapped, struggling with her lack of self-confidence.

"Ivy, wait up!"

She heard the voice and felt sick for a minute as she turned to see Henry Blackwell jogging her way in dress shoes, dress pants, and a white dress shirt. She saw him so differently now. She waited as he approached and took in his neatness and her lack of any attraction. He wasn't Chris. She said nothing.

"Heard you called in sick yesterday," he said. "I meant to call and check up on you, see if you were all right, and make sure everything between us is okay." He gestured at her, and what could she say to him after what he'd done? *Yeah, sure, scumbag. Everything is fine.* She was grateful she stopped herself before saying something really stupid.

Then he touched her shoulder, and her eyes went right there. His touch was something she didn't want. Maybe he figured that out, as he dropped his hand. "Look, I'm so sorry, and I'm still kicking myself for what happened. I shouldn't have done a lot of things, but you have to know everything I did was for you and what I believe was in your best interest."

There it was again: deciding for her.

"Well, that's the thing, Henry. I decide what's best for me, not you," she said, and he lifted his hand.

"Got it, and I deserve that, but, Ivy, we've known each other a long time, worked together, and I truly have feelings for you," he said. She was shaking her head and wanted him to stop, and maybe he knew, as he touched her lips with his finger. "Just hear me out. I just want to make it up to you for what I did. I overstepped, and I'm sorry."

She was a little surprised by his sincerity. "Okay, it's fine, Henry, forgotten, and you don't need to make anything up to me. Let's just let bygones be bygones and move on. I really have to get in there. My shift is about to start." She gestured at the door and met his smile. It was soft, the one she remembered from the Henry she'd hung around with, drinking with him and the other hospital staff.

"I'll walk you in, if that's all right," he said.

"Sure."

He held the door open for her and strode across the lobby to the elevator. "So I really hope you are feeling well, or was it because of me that you called in sick yesterday?"

He reached around her and jabbed the elevator button to go up.

"Not to worry, I'm fine. I drove to Kansas to see Chris." She took in the surprise on his face and then something else he quickly masked.

"Oh well, I see. So are you two…?" He left the question hanging as the door opened. She stepped in, and he followed and jabbed the button to the maternity ward. The doors closed.

This time she turned to Henry and faced him. "Yes, we are, Henry, together. We're just sorting out logistics right now, but Chris and I are very much together."

She didn't expect Henry to smile, and as soon as she said it, she wished she could take it back. He crossed his arms and looked down at her as if trying to figure something out. It was unnerving.

"You know what, Ivy? I want to say I'm happy for you, I really do, but my feelings for you are so strong, and I truly believe that not choosing me, being with a guy like Chris, you'll eventually discover has been the biggest mistake of your life."

She wanted to argue with him, and maybe he knew, as he lifted his hand and touched her shoulder so gently this time before pulling back.

"Just hear me out, Ivy. As your friend, I feel I need to tell you this, because yeah, the guy's hot, but you'll wake up—maybe not tomorrow or even next month but a year or five down the road—and you'll realize you traded in something that could have been real and substantial and lasted a lifetime for something that was all about chemistry and didn't stand a chance of going the distance. Guys like Chris aren't made like you and I are, Ivy. You may not be able to see it right now, but you're smart, and I'm pretty sure, deep down, you know I'm right."

The door slid open, and people were waiting to get in. As she stepped out of the elevator and turned left to the maternity ward, Henry headed down the hall and pushed open the door to the doctors' lounge. She found herself standing there for a minute just staring at the closed door.

"You're wrong, Henry," she said out loud, forcing away all the doubts he'd tried to plant in her head.

Chapter Twenty-Eight

Chris was a smalltime metal fabricator with seven employees, six of them men in the warehouse and only one a woman who handled everything in his office. Betty had dark hair, was in her thirties, and was divorced, with two young girls—and she had to be wondering what the hell was going on.

He'd called in the two idiots who had delivered the flatbed of goods to the client, and of course they'd apologized, felt like crap, and sworn up a blue streak about the man who'd looked them in the eye and promised to have the check in the morning. The problem was that while Chris's bank manager had been sympathetic about the situation, the expected payment that was now a loss, he hadn't granted Chris an extension on the amount owing.

As he leaned back in his chair, taking in his tiny grimy office at the back of the concrete block warehouse he rented, Chris struggled to figure out how to clean up this mess.

"Hey, boss, you okay?"

There was a knock on the door, and he swiveled around to see Betty and the way she worried her lip. She was nice, and he could tell she knew some of what had happened.

He gestured for her to come in. "Sorry about this, Betty. Shitty day. Still can't believe those two numbskulls left the order. I should have been here. This is entirely on me—especially the size of that order."

She stepped inside and then did something she normally didn't: She closed the door. When she turned back to him, he could see something was on her mind. "I don't know if I should say this, but just yesterday I had this feeling that something wasn't quite right when they came back and said they didn't get the check. They said he'd forgotten it and talked up how it would have been a waste of time to load the units back up and bring them all back in the morning. He promised them he'd have the check first thing, and I know Greg and Turner. They were worried about what you'd say. When they went first thing in the morning and discovered what happened, how the client wasn't going to pay, I know they were sick. They're both worried you're going to fire them. I guess I'm in here to plead their cases, but at the same time I have to ask how this loss will affect things here..." She trailed off. He suspected she had to be worried about him meeting payroll. The money did trickle down.

"You don't need to worry about your paycheck," he said. "I'm trying to get things sorted out here, and to be honest, this loss hurts, but I'm not out of options." Yes, he just had to take stock of his assets, his house, truck, tools... What could he mortgage, lien? Add to that the problem that everything always came due at the same time.

"Okay, but I have two girls, and I depend on this job to

pay my rent, buy food. You know that, so if something changes, you'll tell me?" she said.

He knew she was pleading with him not to leave her high and dry. He leaned forward. "Betty, whatever happened is on me. You have nothing to worry about, and if there is something, you have my word I'll tell you," he said and took in the relief in her expression. "Seriously, I promise you I will sort out this mess. I won't leave you high and dry."

She firmed her lips, smiled, and then touched the door. "Okay, thank you. Is there anything I can do, though?"

The phone started ringing again. "No, just tell anyone else who calls for me today that I'm not available and take a message. Stall them, tell them I'm in a meeting and won't be getting back to anyone until tomorrow."

"You got it," she said and hurried back out. She lifted the receiver, and he could hear her doing just what he'd asked.

He thought of Naomi and her dad's suggestion, which he was pretty sure was actually a decree that she'd down-played. Move to Wyoming, stay in Taz's cabin, and, what, hold hands and sneak around? It was absurd, just one more thing on his plate that had gone from easy to unman-ageable. He knew he needed to call her as he stared at the messages already piled on his desk—his supplier demanding payment, a charity he'd donated to already, and three clients who owed him money he had every inten-tion of collecting.

He knew what he wanted to have with Ivy, but he'd have to wait until he could make some sense of the mess of his business and his life. He lifted his phone, wondering who he could call next, when his cell phone started ringing again. Ivy's name flashed on the screen. As he lifted the phone, he stared at the icon for a second ring. He hesitated, then pressed decline and set it back down. Shutting his eyes for a second, he leaned back in his chair, wondering how he was going to dig himself out of this mess.

Chapter Twenty-Nine

Now what?

She paced the floor in her kitchen after calling Chris. It had gone to voicemail yet again, but this time his mailbox had been full. So he wasn't even checking his messages. That had her heart sinking a little more at the thought that Henry could in any way be right about Chris. He'd promised to call her back this morning, and here it was, after nine in the evening. The sun had set.

"Well, maybe you're just not cut out for this, Ivy," she said to herself. "He had a change of heart. You weren't in too deep, so you just need to pull on your big-girl pants, get up tomorrow and go to work, and write this off as…" She stopped talking. The pep talk only made the giant ache worse.

So she pulled open the freezer and spotted a cold carton of double chocolate fudge. Her hand lingered on it. She shouldn't. "Shut up," she said to her head as she gave in and reached for the carton. She pulled it out and then grabbed a spoon from the drawer, seeing as the ice cream was already half gone. She dug in, and the first bite tasted like heaven. There was a knock on her door.

"Come in," she called out over her shoulder as she strode into the living room and plopped down on the sofa, pulling her legs up under her. "Hey, Dad," she said to her father as he strode in, wearing blue jeans and a faded T-shirt, his dark hair thick and graying and in need of a trim.

"Just wanted to stop in and check on you after last night. You kind of left this morning without a word, and we're not sure where you and Chris are at."

She couldn't believe her dad was the one asking, because this was more something her mother did. She shoveled another spoonful in her mouth, and she could see her dad taking it in, but he, unlike her sisters, said nothing. "Me neither, to tell you the truth. I've talked to him only once and told him what you said about moving here. He said nothing except that he'd call me back, and he hasn't, so either he's decided I'm too much work and he's going to cut his losses, or the problems at his job site are worse than he let on."

Her dad frowned. She hadn't told him about that. She lifted her spoon again and swallowed a big chunk, instantly getting a brain freeze. She winced, touched her temple and rubbed, and then proceeded to dig in for more.

"What problems?" he said.

"Chris got a call yesterday morning, some trouble at a job site, a client. I guess there was a pretty big order, a hundred grand or so, he said, and the client didn't pay and now has no intention of paying because everything got damaged. I could tell Chris was really thrown by it all," she said, and her dad was still watching her.

"The way that young man came after you and worried about you, Ivy, he isn't the type to just walk away like you said, and I think you know that. But I am surprised he'd give credit to a client like that for that kind of amount. That's just bad business and not a smart way to run a company," her dad added, and that made her mad, so she jabbed her spoon into the ice cream.

"He didn't give credit. It was some guys who worked for him and were talked into it by the client. Chris was here because of me when he should have been there looking after his business. I feel so bad because I think this is my fault." She touched her forehead again, unable to shake the feeling that something bad was coming her way. "I don't know what to do. I've called and called him today, but he hasn't called me back, and now his voicemail is full. What am I supposed to do?" She dumped the carton of ice cream on the table as her dad walked in and took a seat on the chair across from her. He was looking around as if trying to think of what to say.

"Well, I tell you what you don't do. Give up. It's different for him now. He's got a world of responsibility on him, holding things down. I know Chris has worked real hard for what he built, so I can imagine what this is doing to him. If it was his people who messed up, he's still responsible."

In a way, it made sense.

"So what do I do, wait?"

Her dad nodded. "Well, yeah, Ivy. That's all you can do. He'll call, and him not calling back now doesn't mean he doesn't care. It just means he's got a bunch of things he's got to deal with, so give him some time. Space is sometimes what a man needs to figure things out." Then her dad stood up, but she wanted more.

"And how much time is that?" she said.

He stopped at the door and turned back to her. The way he said nothing, she could tell he was thinking. He shrugged. "I don't know, Ivy, but you've called, and he knows you've called, so you need to give him time to figure things out."

He stepped out and pulled the door closed behind him, and Ivy wanted to scream, because that told her nothing. She didn't feel any better, so she reached for the carton and poked the spoon around. She took one more bite before lifting out the spoon, walking to the trash, and dumping what was left in the carton into the garbage.

Eating her way out of a broken heart only widened her thighs and gave her a bigger ass. Maybe she should take up jogging.

Chapter Thirty

"Ivy, listen. I'm sorry I haven't called, but things have been kind of a mess here. I'm still sorting it out, though, and I'll call you again." He let the receiver dip away from his lips as he finished the pathetic message on her voicemail. Then he hung up and dumped his phone on his table.

Of course she was mad. She had every right to be, considering he hadn't called her back yesterday at all, but he'd been so focused on trying to salvage his business. One loss of a huge order, over a hundred and twenty grand and change, was one thing, but his inability to order any new supplies to cover the upcoming two orders which he needed to break even at the end of the week had put him one step closer to everything collapsing around him. If he couldn't fulfill these orders, he'd lose the business. Word would get out, and his already struggling company would be on the rocks. His kitchen table was littered with paper, his computer was open, and he had a list started to figure out what he could liquidate.

His house was mortgaged, his truck wasn't worth

enough, his line of credit was maxed out, and his credit card had maybe ten thousand to play with. What the hell was he going to do?

Then his cell phone rang. He didn't think as he answered, "Chris here." He needed a shower and some fresh air to clear his head.

"Robert Parker. Chris, do you have a minute?"

Not who he'd been expecting.

"Sure. Listen, I just tried calling Ivy…"

"Not what I was calling about, but good to hear. I know she's been pretty worried, thinking you had a change of heart."

He could hear something in the background, but he didn't know for sure what it was. Traffic maybe, a vehicle running. "No, of course I didn't have a change of heart. How could she think that?" Dealing with Ivy's insecurities was way down on his list of things he was even remotely willing to jump into right now.

"Well, when you don't call back, it's kind of what women do. They start thinking up all the reasons, logical or not—but, again, not really why I'm calling. I wanted to sit down with you, have a talk."

Exactly what he didn't need right now. "You know, I would, but right now I kind of have my hands full dealing with a situation."

"I'm aware," Robert said, and now he wondered how much Ivy had shared. The last thing he wanted was anyone sticking their nose into his business and seeing how many ways he'd fucked up.

"I see. So Ivy is also sharing my personal business. No, I don't have time to come back there and meet with you. I need to be here to fix this mess that happened because I was away in another state instead of taking care of a contract." He was shaking his head and wanted to say a few things to Ivy.

"Don't be mad at her. She's just worried. Listen, I have some idea of what's happening and wouldn't ask you to come out here right now, so I'm on my way to Kansas."

So that was what he was hearing in the background. "You're driving here now?"

"I am, about halfway there, so can you make time?"

What was he supposed to say, no? Even though he was of a mind to.

He gave Robert Parker his address and hung up, expecting him by early afternoon, which gave him enough time now to shower, get a few hours' sleep, and hope for some miracle that would save his ass.

"PRETTY IMPRESSIVE WHAT YOU HAVE HERE," Robert Parker said, looking around the industrial metal fabrication building. Chris was at least thankful the man understood some of the complexity of assembling, cutting, and bending metal to make different structures. His current project was heating ducts, and Robert was looking around at the now empty shop. Of course his employees were long gone.

"Thanks," Chris said. To him, the place had always seemed more impressive than it did now. He said nothing else, not wanting to talk.

"Any way you're going to be able to dig yourself out of this mess?" Robert asked, both hands on his hips. The man was sizing him up.

"I don't know. The fact is that I dropped the ball. I knew the mistake I made. It was my responsibility, and I should have been here to handle this client. I'd have collected before anything was unloaded. Now…" He looked around at the unfinished work. "We needed to have all this finished today and be ready to start our next order tomorrow, but I can't even get an extension from the bank or credit for more supplies, considering the loss I just took."

"What about the client who owes you? What're the chances you'll get paid?"

There was an echo in the building when it was empty, and he found himself looking up at the mottled pipes. "Could hire a lawyer and sue him, and I'd win, but collecting is a whole other thing, especially if he goes out of business or files for bankruptcy. It all comes down to me being able to pay for a lawyer to sue him to begin with. He's most likely counting on the fact that I can't, and he's right." Now he was out of options. He had payroll to meet, suppliers to pay, and bills due and not enough to cover everything.

"It's a bad position to be in." Robert was running his hand over a piece of equipment as if he could see himself there, or maybe it was something else. "A lot of things can go wrong at any time, some big and some small. Sometimes you find a way to dig out of it. I hope you do, for your sake, but Ivy can't sit on the sidelines forever and wait for you to figure things out. She's got a great career, and her quitting and moving here and hoping to pick something up isn't smart on her part. You think you can fix this mess?"

He wanted to say yes, but he couldn't get his tongue to move.

Robert stepped to him and rested a hand on his shoulder. "I like you, Chris, I do, but I'm not having a daughter of mine packing up and leaving for something that may or may not work. You have some real problems you need to fix here. Sort out your business, and then come and talk to Ivy again. Work out something a little more manageable."

What he meant by that, Chris wasn't sure. "Is this about keeping your daughter close? I know Taz is living with Jerry in Denver…" He stopped as Robert shook his head and lifted his hand.

"There's a difference there. Jerry has means, and while I'm not happy with Taz being so far away, it's a different situation. So is it with her other sister Brandyne."

He had to think for a minute. Ah, yes, the one married to the Montana sheriff. "So it's about the money?"

Robert was shaking his head. "It's about being settled, Chris. You're not settled, Ivy is, and this has been far too quick for my liking. Take some time, get things sorted out. You and Ivy can visit, and if it's really meant to work, it will," her father said. He wondered why it seemed he was pushing him away.

"So the call I had from Ivy, she said you insisted I move to Wyoming, live at Taz's…" He didn't need to finish, as Robert was shaking his head again.

"Let's not rush things and be too hasty. Get yourself sorted here first." He lifted his hand to the warehouse, taking everything in, and then slapped Chris on the arm as he walked past. "Let me know if there's anything I can do, but a word of advice, Chris." Robert stopped a little ways away.

Chris said nothing as he waited for the man to say his peace.

"Be kind to Ivy. Don't string her along. Maybe take a break for a bit until you finish getting yourself together. She doesn't need to be cleaning up your mess."

Then he walked off, and Chris felt as if Ivy had already slipped away.

Chapter Thirty-One

It had been five days since her dad had told her he'd driven to Kansas and had a sit down with Chris, and it had been four since she'd received a voicemail from Chris telling her that he needed some time to sort out his mess. It was a call she hadn't returned, because she'd figured that was his way of saying, *So long, take care. It's been fun.*

Added to that was that Henry had dropped his interest in her completely, having found new prey. She'd spotted him with a different nurse from Pediatrics, and as of three days ago he'd treated her as if she were just any other nurse in the maternity ward and didn't exist. It was odd and should have been welcome except for the fact that she was very much alone now, having gone from two men to none.

"What are you doing?" Naomi said. It startled her, and she jumped from where she'd been lacing up her new sneakers after pulling on new jogging capris and squeezing her larger bust into a sports bra with a loose tank overtop.

Her hair was in a ponytail, and she put her foot to the dirt and switched to her other sneaker, tightening the laces.

"Going for a run," she said as if this were perfectly normal. She'd hired a trainer in Buffalo and had started working out five days earlier the morning after she'd dumped the last tub of ice cream she was ever planning to eat in the trash. That was something she'd shared with no one.

"I see. Actually, I don't. Since when do you run?" Naomi asked. She was wearing a spotted blue sundress and had the perfect slim figure guys loved. Her long hair was braided down her back, and her blue eyes were shocked—no, horrified, staring at Ivy through dark-rimmed glasses. So much for support. Maybe that was why she'd decided not to share her new fitness regime with anyone.

"I just started. Decided to take back all of me and take some of my own advice. If I don't like me, then change it. So this is the new me." She gestured to her size, thinking of her new meal plan, which didn't include biscuits, gravy, or anything fried, so no more dinner at her parents'. Sunday dinner, she'd have to bring her own, and everyone would just have to get used to the idea or she would be just fine with eating alone.

Naomi was still gaping and standing there, but Ivy had a driveway she was determined to run. She'd run sixty seconds on, two minutes off, following her trainer's program. Her body would ache, and she'd be out of breath and hate every minute of it, but she was determined to get to her goal.

"Okay, gotta go," she said. "As much as I'd rather sit and chit chat, I have some sweating to do."

"Wait! Wow, that's great. Maybe I should ask how you're doing. Is this because of Chris, this…?" She gestured to her size-twelve plumpness squeezed into her new athletic gear. Yup, Ivy was so done talking about this.

"You know what, Naomi? As much as you may think otherwise, what I'm doing is for me and no one else. Not some guy, not you—me. And, as a matter of fact, I'm also really tired of the comments from my sisters and the looks you all keep giving me about my size. Well, Scarlett for sure is nasty to just about everyone, but you and even Taz, I've seen the way you take in my increasing size. You may not say anything, but the way you stare at me, watch me at times, says everything, and I'm tired of it. It hurts. Mason is the only one who doesn't see me any differently. And in case you didn't know, Chris and I are over." She flipped her hand in the air and took in the sadness staring back at her. Good grief, she hated the pity look, and it was starting to piss her off. "Look, can you and your perfect body just go on back to your cottage and leave me be?" She stepped down and took a step away before a hand touched her arm.

"Ivy, please. That's not what I meant. I guess I want to apologize and say I'm sorry it didn't work out with Chris. I really liked him and thought he was so good for you, and I never meant to make you feel less than because of your weight. I'm sorry for making you feel that way."

She felt the emotion well in her chest. She'd never expected this apology and kindness, not when she was doing everything she could to hold it all together, so she had to clear her throat.

Then she heard a vehicle. Stepping around her car, she saw a truck coming, an older model, and a man behind the wheel that looked so much like Chris. It was a pickup, faded brown, and he was in shades as he pulled up beside her car and parked.

She was staring at him as he climbed out, looking like

perfection in faded jeans and a washed-out T-shirt. He glanced once to Naomi, who was still standing there but made an excuse and walked away. Ivy said nothing as she stayed right where she was.

"Hi," he said, pulling off his shades and tucking them in his shirtfront.

"Hi yourself," she said, wanting to walk closer and press her hand to his chest, to touch him, but she willed herself to stay where she was. *Don't be one of those women.*

Silence and heaviness lingered between them, and there was something in his expression she didn't quite understand, but she wasn't going to ask.

Chris moved, taking a step toward her and then another before stopping in front of her, looking down at her as a subtle smile touched his lips. "I'm sorry for everything I've made a mess of," he said. "I've closed up shop, paid my employees, and sold everything to pay off what I owed, so I'm here now to start fresh."

Damn, he was handsome, and she wasn't sure she'd heard him right.

"Let me get this straight," she said. "Your business…"

"Is gone, folded. It was a hole so deep I couldn't get out of it. I lost enough sleep trying to fix a mess and getting nowhere, so I found a buyer for my house and my truck. All I had left was enough to buy this thing and the boxes in back."

She took in the truck and the boxes she hadn't seen, and she realized what he was saying. "You're here for…"

"You," he said as he stepped in, sliding his hand over her bare arms. Then he stepped back and took in her outfit. "What's this?"

"Jogging, getting into shape—but I don't understand. I called, and the last message I had from you, I thought that was it."

"No, the message said I needed to clean things up, and I did. Now I'm here for you. Well, we are," he said.

"We?" she said as he stepped to the truck cab and pulled open the door.

He lifted out a cat carrier holding the mangy black cat she'd seen at his place. "Yeah, we. We're kind of a package deal. If you'll have us," he said, putting the carrier on the step.

This time she went to him. His arms slid around her and lifted her as he pressed his lips to hers. The kiss was everything.

"And these, they're going to be so much fun to peel off you." He ran his hand over her ass as she heard the door of her parents' house, and they both glanced over to see her parents there watching. This time her dad was smiling.

"My dad…" she started as she turned back to Chris. He put her down.

"That's a conversation I need to have, but it's not going to be a problem. I love you, and we're going to be together. Here. We'll figure it out, you and me, okay?" he said.

She looked around Chris again, seeing her dad lift his hand, slip his arm over her mother's shoulder, and walk back into the house. "Yeah," she said. "You and me."

Turn the page for a sneak peek of
PLAYING HARD TO GET the next book in *THE PARKER SISTERS*
Available in eBook, Audio and Paperback

A journalist chasing a big story. The corrupt, powerful subject she's out to expose. But what if the truth about him turns her life upside down?

Playing Hard to Get

CHAPTER 1

S taring at her unfamiliar image in the mirror was both exciting and shocking. Naomi Parker had never been blond, sultry, a walking sex kitten—and without glasses. But that was in fact the image before her now. It gave her a thrill. She was living on the edge, becoming someone she was born to be deep down, playing a part that was dangerous but would solidify Naomi for who she really was, a rockstar journalist who would uncover anything and everything that no one else could.

Just as quickly as the thought excited her, it worried her, because unfortunately her parents, Robert and Susan, and her sisters had no idea what she'd gotten herself into. If they found out this side of her that she hid from everyone, well, let's just say she hated to think what their response would be—after the shock wore off, that is. Something close to "Over my dead body" or "Hell no," with a dash of "What were you thinking?" and, to finish it off, "How do we get her out of this mess so she'll again be the daughter we raised her to be?"

To Naomi, though, it wasn't a mess or a pending disaster. She was chasing the story of a lifetime, a story no one else would touch, about a man with a sordid past. A monster, according to the people of Casper, Wyoming, with his bad attitude, dangerous good looks, linebacker build, and eyes that could stop a woman cold. Not that she knew what that meant, but Naomi had every intention of exposing Cameron Donnelly for the lying, cheating fraud he was, for an abuser of power who'd dominated the local headlines just one year earlier. He was all everyone could talk about and had become the man you didn't want to be associated with.

How she was going to do that was still forming in her mind, but she could feel the sizzle of this new Naomi— oops, or rather, Julie, with her bleached hair, colored contact lenses making her blue eyes even bluer, heavy shadow and thick mascara that made them pop, and a C-cup push-up bra providing cleavage and a bold display of her assets, something she'd never have dared show anyone, under a barely decent slimming silky tank and indecently short skirt with four-inch spike heels.

Yes, it was perfect, exactly the kind of woman that would have Cameron drooling, chasing her down, and spilling all his secrets. She heard the toilet flush and took in the stall door that opened. The woman had short dark hair, a mass of curls, a short knit skirt that appeared painted on, spike heels, and a skintight tank showing her generous bust. Yes, she definitely fit in.

"I swear these shoes are going to be the end of me, but the guys love 'em. Gets me those big tips, so I guess in the end it's worth it, although not sure my feet think the same." She had a deep, husky voice and was wiping a dark smudge under her eye from her thick mascara. Then she turned, giving Naomi a view of her curvy body and the way the skirt eased over her rounded butt and mile-long legs. The woman didn't just have a great figure; she had muscle and was perfectly toned. She winked at Naomi. "You one of the new girls?"

It took her a minute as she started to sweat. "Hoping to be. I'm here to meet with Pete. Although I don't have a lot of experience waiting tables, I really need the work," she said, cringing, realizing she may have gone a little overboard. She hoped it didn't sound too desperate.

The woman rolled her eyes and crossed her arms. "You should fit right in. Not to worry. It's about the looks, honey. Everything else can be taught." She gestured to Naomi's getup. "Yup, one look at you and the interview will be over." She leaned in the mirror again, dragging a deep red painted nail under her eye as if there was something there. "Just flash him a smile, and if you need to, tell him you've waited tables before over in Rock Springs. Can't see it getting that far, though. Pete's about the looks and whether you've got the heat and can sell it. Just let him get an eyeful of that cleavage and you'll be a shoe in."

She tapped the counter. "Just a word of advice, hon: If you really want to work here, the pay isn't great. If that's what you're counting on, go get a job at Smitty's family restaurant down the road. Here it's about the tips, which are exceptional, but it comes at a cost. The men providing said tips are pigs coming in off the rigs and are as free with their hands as they are with their wallets. As long as you understand that, you'll do just fine. Taffy is my name," she said, leaning against the counter. Of course she was waiting for something from Naomi.

"Julie," she spat out, feeling her heart kick up from the lie that had begun. She should have put more thought into it. Julie what? Her hands were sweaty. Her adrenaline surged.

"Nice to meet you, Julie. Hope you get the job," Taffy said before leaving.

Naomi took one last look in the mirror, lifted the strap of her small clutch over her shoulder, and said, "Show time."

She'd practiced walking in these spike heels for days, but she teetered a second as she took a step. Maybe getting the job wouldn't be the challenge; it would be staying upright in these ridiculously high shoes.

THE MUSIC WAS PULSING EVEN through the closed door of the back office. The room was ordinary, with an old scratched-up desk, a small steel safe in the corner, and an old four-drawer file cabinet. Turned out the man was named Dean, not Pete. The only thing she'd figured out was that he used to play sports, either a former boxer or hockey player, she couldn't remember which he'd said when she'd first stumbled in, reeling at the change in script. She'd done her homework on Pete and was thrown. Thinking on her feet wasn't really her strong suit. That was her sister Scarlett, who was a pain in the ass but had a skill Naomi coveted.

"So you've worked for Mr. Donnelly for how long?" Naomi said.

Dean didn't look up from where he rested his forearms on the desk, a pen in hand, writing something in a note-book. It was odd. He set the pen down and leaned back in the heavily padded older chair. It squeaked. His face was free of emotion and hard. Yikes!

"Why is it that I'm starting to feel as if I'm the one being interviewed?" He was studying her, and she didn't have a clue whether he was amused or ready to tell her to get lost.

She swallowed. Things were fast spiraling to the edge of a precipice where one of two things would happen: The opportunity she'd only just stepped into would be gone or, by some miracle, she'd get a pass. Unfortunately, she realized it would likely be the former, and that had her mind reeling, grasping at anything instead of remaining calm so she could nail this interview.

"Sorry, just curious. Always have been," she said. "Guess it's one of my faults. I tend to ask questions when nervous." She was sitting ramrod straight, her chest out, and sweat was dripping from her underarms. She leaned forward, going right to plan C, giving him an eyeful. He didn't seem interested at all. It was as if he was completely unaffected by her. He had to be a monk, or maybe it was the fact that Naomi didn't have a clue how to entice a guy. None of this was the reaction she'd expected. She was completely out of her element. She was drowning and sinking fast.

He lifted his pen again, and she could see the neat penmanship from where she sat. Odd for a guy to be focused on so much detail. "So you've waited tables in Rock Creek, where?" Direct and to the point.

She felt her throat close up and tried to think of all the places in Rock Creek, a place she'd been to only a handful of times. She couldn't remember the name of one damn place. "Bottoms Up," she finally said, recalling the roadside sign of a half-naked country gal with cutoffs that showed off more of her rounded ass than they covered. She was proud of herself and smiled brightly as she wrapped her hands over her crossed legs, just barely stopping herself from batting her lashes.

The man looked up. He had blue eyes and hair so short

it was almost buzzed. This time he smiled. His eyes danced, and her stomach knotted, because something wasn't right. "Yeah?" He actually laughed, controlled and rough, and she could feel her jaw tighten as he flicked the pen in his fingers and leaned back again, the smile now gone. "So when exactly was this?" He clicked the pen a couple more times, and her eyes went right there.

She was in a panic, in shock, and for a minute she thought she might puke from her nerves as she searched her mind for something, anything. "Two, three months ago." Her voice squeaked, completely rattled now. "I was at a small coffeehouse before that…"

His gaze was so deep. "Why is it that I think you're trying to blow smoke up my ass? I know everyone who works and has worked at Bottoms Up for the last five years, and, sweetheart, that ain't you." He wasn't smiling now, and his eyes had a look that said she was fucking with the wrong guy. "Coming in here and wasting my time by lying through your teeth to get a job, I ain't got time for that kind of bullshit." He gestured with his pen to a sign hammered to the wall, a drawing of a stickman in a hangman's noose. Below was written in red, *What happens to liars!*

It was something she'd never seen before, and her face flamed as she glanced back to him, wide eyed, seeing him organized and stacking papers into a pile, knowing he was so done with her.

"Word of advice," he said. "If you're going to lie, at least do your fucking homework and don't pick a business owned by Mr. Donnelly." He then winked, set his pen down, and lifted both hands, putting his fingers together. It was a move she found intimidating. Oh, good Lord, she was so screwed. Now what?

"Okay, I'm sorry, I lied. The problem is that I've never waited a table before in my life, unless you count dinner at my parents', where I clear dirty dishes and put food on the table, which I've done countless times." She uncrossed her legs and slid to the edge of the chair, her hands on the edge of the desk as desperation now threatened to strangle her. "I just really need this job and know places won't hire unless you have experience, but how am I supposed to get experience if you won't give me a chance? Please." Her voice squeaked. She was considering getting down on her knees and begging, anything to get him to look at her or at least give her one more chance, feeling the door closing on any chance of getting close to Cameron Donnelly. The man was untouchable, and the opening was closing before her. She'd never get another shot.

No such luck. The man was made of steel as if he didn't have an ounce of compassion for anyone. In fact, he was shaking his head, his expression set, as he started to lean forward to stand up. Next she knew, she'd be dismissed and the door would slam shut in her face.

Then the door at her back opened, and Cameron Donnelly, six foot two, with lean muscle, impeccably groomed, and better looking in person, if that was possible, stepped in. It was one of those moments where everything happened at once. He took in the room with his shrewd gaze, wondering yet knowing at the same time. His shirtsleeves were rolled up, and the top buttons of his crisp white dress shirt were undone. He oozed something that had Naomi struggling to take a breath. How was it possible a man could affect her this way? Then she realized as she beamed up at him that he hadn't given her a second glance.

"I need you over in Laramie tomorrow," he said. "Handle the partners meeting for me. Make sure no issues arise this time." He pulled keys from the desk drawer and lifted a suit jacket she hadn't seen hanging from a hook on the wall. It was black and tailored and fit him like a glove. He still hadn't looked her way, not a glance, nothing, not an acknowledgement that she existed. Odd, considering how hot she looked. That definitely didn't help her confidence.

"Just finishing here now so I can be on my way…" Dean said. He lifted his wrist, glancing at his watch. "I'd say fifteen, tops."

"The situation's been handled?" Cameron was pulling at his cuffs.

Both men were carrying on as if she didn't even exist. It was so cryptic, and she wished she'd thought to record this. Her cell phone was slipped in her handbag, and it would be so easy to feign a call and turn it on. Then both men were staring at her. Cameron cleared his throat, not a smile, nothing. It really had a way of making a girl feel she wasn't wanted.

Dean stood up. The man was tall, handsome in a hard sort of way but not even close to oozing the attraction that seemed to make up Cameron Donnelly. No wonder women flocked to him. Fell prey to him.

"Thank you for coming, Miss…." Dean didn't offer his hand, and she knew in that panicked second she was being dismissed.

"Parker, Julie Parker. Please, I know I shouldn't have said I had experience and that I worked at a place I haven't, but I swear if you give me a chance, you won't regret it. I'm a quick learner, and I'll work hard."

Cameron glanced once to Dean and said only "You got this?" Then he started to the door.

This was going from bad to worse, and she had about half a second, she figured, before her opportunity was gone forever. She didn't think, she reacted. She jumped from the chair, swaying on those ridiculous heels and reaching out. She touched his arm, feeling the expensive dark cloth of his suit jacket. His eyes went to her hand, and she felt him flinch from her touch—something else she hadn't expected. He didn't look at her until she pulled her hand away. His eyes were green, an odd shade, and there was nothing friendly there. He was hard, unforgiving, alpha, and she was so screwed.

"Please, Mr. Donnelly, give me a chance. I promise you will not regret this. A week. One week! One day! And then if I don't show you I can do a good job, you can let me go." She was usually more convincing, but he was giving her nothing.

He glanced over her head to Dean, and they exchanged a look.

"She lied," Dean said. "Was just about to explain the policy." He gestured again to the homemade sign.

Cameron was looking straight through her as if she didn't exist. "I don't like liars and don't want the kind of trouble that always comes with a liar." He gestured to the open door and started to step away.

This was now at the stage where she was so fucking screwed that pride and dignity didn't have a place anymore. "I get it, and I never planned to come in and lie and say I had experience, but I was also expecting to be interviewed by Pete, who would have been more interested in how I looked and how much skin I showed. My experience wouldn't have been something that mattered… I'm not a liar, I don't lie, but I really need this job." She was rambling, and her face was burning under all the caked-on makeup that made her eyes itch. She wondered for a moment whether they could see through some of her half-truths, her lies, and all the bullshit she was tossing out to turn the tables so this would go her way.

Cameron still hadn't moved. He was watching her, and

she didn't have a fucking clue what the hell he was thinking. That had the sweat beading between her shoulder blades.

"One day then, please," she said. "I beg you, give me a chance. I swear I'm a hard worker. You won't regret it."

The silence continued. It was only her panicked breath she could hear. She watched as Cameron wiped his face, and all that she could think was that he appeared tired. She didn't have a clue whether she'd gotten through to him. Maybe he'd have her thrown out now with a warning never to come back.

"Don't do it," she heard Dean say from behind her just as Cameron stepped out the door.

He then turned back to them, his hand in the air, his eyes closed a second before looking over to Dean. "Give her the job, but if she pulls anything, get rid of her." Then he was gone without looking her way or giving her anything to say, "Okay, I see you."

Lies, deception, greed. Yes, she wasn't being honest, but then, he was all of that and more. He deserved to be exposed, and Naomi Parker had no doubt now that she'd be able to scrape together the story that would officially take Cameron Donnelly down.

About the Author

"Lorhainne Eckhart is one of my go to authors when I want a guaranteed good book. So many twists and turns, but also so much love and such a strong sense of family."

(Lora W., Reviewer)

New York Times & USA Today bestseller Lorhainne Eckhart is best known for her writing Raw Relatable Real Romances, where "Morals and family are running themes. Danger, romance, and a drive to do what is right will see you glued to the page." As one fan calls her, she is the "Queen of the family saga." (aherman) writing "the ups and downs of what goes on within a family but also with some suspense, angst and of course a bit of romance thrown in for good measure." Follow Lorhainne on Bookbub to receive alerts on New Releases and Sales and join her mailing list at LorhainneEckhart.com for her Monday Blog, books news, giveaways and FREE reads. With over 120 books, audiobooks, and multiple series published and available at all retailers now translated into six languages. She is a multiple recipient of the Readers' Favorite Award for Suspense and Romance, and lives in the Pacific Northwest on an island, is the mother of three, her oldest has autism and she is an advocate for never giving up on your dreams.

"Lorhainne Eckhart has this uncanny way of just hitting the spot every time with her books."

(Caroline L., Reviewer)

The O'Connells: *The O'Connells of Livingston, Montana are not your typical family. A riveting collection of stories surrounding the ups and downs of what goes on within a family but also with some suspense, angst and of course a bit of romance thrown in for good measure "I thought I loved the Friessens, but I absolutely adore the O'Connell's. Each and every book has totally different genres of stories but the one thing in common is how she is able to wrap it around the family which is the heart of each story." (C. Logue)*

The Friessens: *An emotional big family romance series, the Friessen family siblings find their relationships tested, lay their hearts on the line, and discover lasting love! "Lorhainne Eckhart is one of my go to authors when I want a guaranteed good book. So many twists and turns, but also so much love and such a strong sense of family." (Lora W., Reviewer)*

The Parker Sisters: *The Parker Sisters are a close-knit family, and like any other family they have their ups and downs. "Eckhart has crafted another intense family drama…The character development is outstanding, and the emotional investment is high…" (Aherman, Reviewer)*

The McCabe Brothers: *Join the five McCabe siblings on their journeys to the dark and dangerous side of love! An intense, exhilarating collection of romantic thrillers you won't want to miss. — "Eckhart has a new series that is definitely worth the read. The queen of the family saga started this series with a spin-off of her wildly successful Friessen series." From a Readers' Favorite award— winning author and "queen of the family saga" (Aherman)*

Billy Jo McCabe Mystery: *The social worker and the cop, an unlikely couple drawn together on a small, secluded Pacific Northwest island where nothing is as it seems. Protecting the innocent comes at a cost, and what seems to be a sleepy, quiet town is anything but.*

Lorhainne loves to hear from her readers! You can connect with me at:
www.LorhainneEckhart.com
lorhainneeckhart.le@gmail.com

 facebook.com/AuthorLorhainneEckhart

 twitter.com/LEckhart

instagram.com/lorhainneeckhart

 bookbub.com/profile/lorhainne-eckhart

 pinterest.com/lorhainneeckhart

The Outsider Series
The Forgotten Child (Brad and Emily)
A Baby and a Wedding *(An Outsider Series Short)*
Fallen Hero (Andy, Jed, and Diana)
The Search *(An Outsider Series Short)*
The Awakening (Andy and Laura)
Secrets (Jed and Diana)
Runaway (Andy and Laura)
Overdue *(An Outsider Series Short)*
The Unexpected Storm (Neil and Candy)
The Wedding (Neil and Candy)

The Friessens: A New Beginning
The Deadline (Andy and Laura)
The Price to Love (Neil and Candy)
A Different Kind of Love (Brad and Emily)
A Vow of Love, A Friessen Family Christmas

The Friessens
The Reunion
The Bloodline (Andy & Laura)
The Promise (Diana & Jed)
The Business Plan (Neil & Candy)
The Decision (Brad & Emily)
First Love (Katy)
Family First
Leave the Light On
In the Moment

In the Family
In the Silence
In the Charm
Unexpected Consequences
It Was Always You
The First Time I Saw You
Welcome to My Arms
Welcome to Boston
I'll Always Love You
Ground Rules
A Reason to Breathe
You Are My Everything
Anything For You
The Homecoming
Stay Away From My Daughter
The Bad Boy
A Place of Our Own
The Visitor
All About Devon
Long Past Dawn
How to Heal a Heart
Keep Me In Your Heart

The O'Connells
The Neighbor
The Third Call
The Secret Husband
The Quiet Day
The Commitment
The Missing Father
The Hometown Hero
Justice
The Family Secret

The Fallen O'Connell
The Return of the O'Connells
And The She Was Gone
The Stalker
The O'Connell Family Christmas
The Girl Next Door

The McCabe Brothers

Don't Stop Me (Vic)
Don't Catch Me (Chase)
Don't Run From Me (Aaron)
Don't Hide From Me (Luc)
Don't Leave Me (Claudia)
Out of Time

A Billy Jo McCabe Mystery

Nothing As it Seems
Hiding in Plain Sight
The Cold Case
The Trap
Above the Law

The Wilde Brothers

The One (Joe and Margaret)
The Honeymoon, A Wilde Brothers Short
Friendly Fire (Logan and Julia)
Not Quite Married, A Wilde Brothers Short
A Matter of Trust (Ben and Carrie)
The Reckoning, A Wilde Brothers Christmas
Traded (Jake)
Unforgiven (Samuel)
The Holiday Bride

Married in Montana
His Promise
Love's Promise
A Promise of Forever

The Parker Sisters
Thrill of the Chase
The Dating Game
Play Hard to Get
What We Can't Have
Go Your Own Way
A June Wedding

Kate & Walker
One Night
Edge of Night
Last Night

Walk the Right Road Series
The Choice
Lost and Found
Merkaba
Bounty
Blown Away: The Final Chapter

The Saved Series
Saved
Vanished
Captured

Single Titles
He Came Back
Loving Christine

For my German Readers
Die Außenseiter-Reihe
Der Vergessene Junge
Der Gefallene Held

For my French Readers
L'ENFANT OUBLIÉ